VARIETIES OF DISTURBANCE

VARIETIES OF DISTURBANCE

stories

LYDIA DAVIS

FARRAR, STRAUS AND GIROUX   NEW YORK

FARRAR, STRAUS AND GIROUX
19 Union Square West, New York 10003

Distributed in Canada by Douglas & McIntyre Ltd.
Printed in the United States of America
First edition, 2007

Grateful acknowledgment is made for permission to reprint the following material:

"Worstward Ho," copyright © 1983 by Samuel Beckett. Used by permission of Grove/Atlantic, Inc.

In "The Walk," quotations from *Swann's Way* by Marcel Proust, copyright © 1978 by Marcel Proust. Used by permission of Modern Library, a division of Random House, Inc.; quotations from *Swann's Way* by Marcel Proust, translated by Lydia Davis, copyright © 2002 by Lydia Davis. Used by permission of Viking Penguin, a division of Penguin Group (USA) Inc.; quotations from *Swann's Way* by Marcel Proust, translated by Lydia Davis, copyright © 2002 by Lydia Davis. Reproduced by permission of Penguin Books Ltd.

Library of Congress Cataloging-in-Publication Data
Davis, Lydia, 1947–
    Varieties of disturbance : stories / Lydia Davis.— 1st ed.
        p.   cm.
    ISBN-13: 978-0-374-28173-1 (hardcover : alk. paper)
    ISBN-10: 0-374-28173-4 (hardcover : alk. paper)
    I. Title.

PS3554.A9356V37 2007
813'.54—dc22

                                            2006033431

Designed by Cassandra J. Pappas

www.fsgbooks.com

3   5   7   9   10   8   6   4

For support during the period in which many of these stories were written, the author would like to thank the John D. and Catherine T. MacArthur Foundation; the State University of New York, Albany, including the College of Arts and Sciences and the Department of English; and the New York State Writers Institute.

for my brother SHD

and for RGD, HHD, and CF,
in loving memory

ACKNOWLEDGMENTS

Grateful acknowledgment is made to the editors of the magazines in which the following stories appeared, sometimes in slightly different form:

32 Poems: "Getting Better," "Two Types"
Avec: "Forbidden Subjects"
American Letters & Commentary: "Her Mother's Mother" (as "Her Mother's Mother: 1," "Her Mother's Mother: 2")
Bomb: "Almost Over: What's the Word?," "A Man from Her Past," "Suddenly Afraid"
Columbia: "Enlightened"
Conjunctions: "Television," "Burning Family Members," "Reducing Expenses"
Fence: "Kafka Cooks Dinner"
Gulf Coast: "The Senses"
Hambone: "20 Sculptures in One Hour," "How It Is Done"
Insurance: "The Way to Perfection"
John Cheney's Literary Magazine: "Television" (sections 1 and 2)
A Little Magazine: "Varieties of Disturbance"

NOON: "Absentminded," "The Caterpillar," "Getting to Know Your Body," "Dog and Me," "Insomnia," "Jane and the Cane," "The Good Taste Contest"

Northern Lit Quarterly: "For Sixty Cents"

Notus: "How She Could Not Drive" (as "Clouds in the Sky")

Quick Fiction: "A Different Man"

Shiny: "Childcare," "Passing Wind," "How Shall I Mourn Them?"

Tolling Elves: "The Busy Road," "The Fellowship" (as "The Fellowship: 1" and "The Fellowship: 2"), "The Fly," "Lonely," "Tropical Storm," excerpts from "What You Learn About the Baby"

The World: "Southward Bound, Reads *Worstward Ho*" (footnotes only, under the title "Going South While Reading *Worstward Ho*"), "My Son"

"Cape Cod Diary" was first published as a pamphlet by Belladonna Books (Brooklyn, 2003)

"Good Times" first appeared in *The Unmade Bed* (ed. Laura Chester; Boston: Faber & Faber, 1992)

"Grammar Questions" first appeared in *110 Stories* (ed. Ulrich Baer; New York: New York University Press, 2002) and was reprinted in *Harper's* ("Readings" section: New York, August 2002)

"How It Is Done" also appeared in *New York Sex* (ed. Jane DeLynn; New York: Painted Leaf Press, 1998)

Some of the material in "Kafka Cooks Dinner" was taken from *Letters to Milena* by Franz Kafka, tr. Philip Boehm (New York: Schocken Books, 1990)

"Southward Bound, Reads *Worstward Ho*" (main text and footnotes, separately) also appeared under the title "Going South, Reads *Worstward Ho*" in Marc Joseph's *New and Used* (London: Steidl Publishing, 2006)

"Television" appeared in *The Pushcart Prize, 1989–1990* (ed. Bill Henderson; New York: Pushcart, 1989)

"Varieties of Disturbance" was reprinted in *Harper's* ("Readings" section: New York, April 1993)

Excerpts from "What You Learn About the Baby" also appeared in *Cradle and All* (ed. Laura Chester; Boston: Faber & Faber, 1989)

CONTENTS

VARIETIES OF
DISTURBANCE

A Man from Her Past

I think Mother is flirting with a man from her past who is not Father. I say to myself: Mother ought not to have improper relations with this man "Franz"! "Franz" is a European. I say she should not see this man improperly while Father is away! But I am confusing an old reality with a new reality: Father will not be returning home. He will be staying on at Vernon Hall. As for Mother, she is ninety-four years old. How can there be improper relations with a woman of ninety-four? Yet my confusion must be this: though her body is old, her capacity for betrayal is still young and fresh.

Dog and Me

An ant can look up at you, too, and even threaten you with its arms. Of course, my dog does not know I am human, he sees me as dog, though I do not leap up at a fence. I am a strong dog. But I do not leave my mouth hanging open when I walk along. Even on a hot day, I do not leave my tongue hanging out. But I bark at him: "No! No!"

Enlightened

I don't know if I can remain friends with her. I've thought and thought about it—she'll never know how much. I gave it one last try. I called her, after a year. But I didn't like the way the conversation went. The problem is that she is not very enlightened. Or I should say, she is not enlightened enough for me. She is nearly fifty years old and no more enlightened, as far as I can see, than when I first knew her twenty years ago, when we talked mainly about men. I did not mind how unenlightened she was then, maybe because I was not so enlightened myself. I believe I am more enlightened now, and certainly more enlightened than she is, although I know it's not very enlightened to say that. But I want to say it, so I am willing to postpone being more enlightened myself so that I can still say a thing like that about a friend.

The Good Taste Contest

The husband and wife were competing in a Good Taste Contest judged by a jury of their peers, men and women of good taste, including a fabric designer, a rare-book dealer, a pastry cook, and a librarian. The wife was judged to have better taste in furniture, especially antique furniture. The husband was judged to have overall poor taste in lighting fixtures, tableware, and glassware. The wife was judged to have indifferent taste in window treatments, but the husband and wife both were judged to have good taste in floor coverings, bed linen, bath linen, large appliances, and small appliances. The husband was felt to have good taste in carpets, but only fair taste in upholstery fabrics. The husband was felt to have very good taste in both food and alcoholic beverages, while the wife had inconsistently good to poor taste in food. The husband had better taste in clothes than the wife though inconsistent taste in perfumes and colognes. While both husband and wife were judged to have no more than fair taste in garden design, they were judged to have good taste in number and variety of evergreens. The husband was felt to have excellent taste in roses but poor taste in bulbs. The wife was felt to have better taste in bulbs and generally good taste in shade plantings with the exception of hostas. The husband's taste was felt to be good in garden furniture but only fair in ornamental planters. The wife's taste was judged consistently poor in garden statuary. After a brief discussion, the judges gave the decision to the husband for his higher overall points score.

Collaboration with Fly

I put that word on the page,
but he added the apostrophe.

Kafka Cooks Dinner

I am filled with despair as the day approaches when my dear Milena will come. I have hardly begun to decide what to offer her. I have hardly confronted the thought yet, only flown around it the way a fly circles a lamp, burning my head over it.

I am so afraid I will be left with no other idea but potato salad, and it's no surprise to her anymore. I mustn't.

The thought of this dinner has been with me constantly all week, weighing on me in the same way that in the deep sea there is no place that is not under the greatest pressure. Now and then I summon all my energy and work at the menu as if I were being forced to hammer a nail into a stone, as if I were both the one hammering and also the nail. But at other times, I sit here reading in the afternoon, a myrtle in my buttonhole, and there are such beautiful passages in the book that I think I have become beautiful myself.

I might as well be sitting in the garden of the insane asylum staring into space like an idiot. And yet I know I will eventually settle on a menu, buy the food, and prepare the meal. In this, I suppose I am like a butterfly: its zigzagging flight is so irregular, it flutters so much it is painful to watch, it flies in what is the very opposite of a straight line, and yet it successfully covers miles and miles to reach its final destination, so it must be more efficient or at least more determined than it seems.

To torture myself is pathetic, too, of course. After all, Alexander didn't torture the Gordian knot when it wouldn't come untied. I feel I am being buried alive under all these thoughts, though at the same time I feel compelled to lie still, since perhaps I am actually dead after all.

This morning, for instance, shortly before waking up, which was also shortly after falling asleep, I had a dream which has not left me yet: I had caught a mole and carried it into the hops field, where it dove into the earth as though into water and disappeared. When I contemplate this dinner, I would like to disappear into the earth like that mole. I would like to stuff myself into the drawer of the laundry chest, and open the drawer from time to time to see if I have suffocated yet. It's so much more surprising that one gets up every morning at all.

I know beet salad would be better. I could give her beets and potatoes both, and a slice of beef, if I include meat. Yet a good slice of beef does not require any side dish, it is best tasted alone, so the side dish could come before, in which case it would not be a side dish but an appetizer. Whatever I do, perhaps she will not think very highly of my effort, or perhaps she will be feeling a little ill to begin with and not stimulated by the sight of those beets. In the case of the first, I would be dreadfully ashamed, and in the case of the second, I would have no advice—how could I?—but just a simple question: would she want me to remove all the food from the table?

Not that this dinner alarms me, exactly. I do after all have some imagination and energy, so perhaps I will be able to make a dinner that she will like. There have been other, passable dinners since the meal I cooked for Felice that was so unfortunate—though perhaps more good than bad came of that one.

It was last week that I invited Milena. She was with a friend. We met by accident on the street and I spoke impulsively. The man with her had a kind, friendly, fat face—a very correct face, as only Germans have. After making the invitation, for a long time I walked through the city as though it were a cemetery, I was so at peace.

Then I began to torment myself, like a flower in a flower box that is thrashed by the wind but loses not a single petal.

Like a letter covered with corrective pencil marks, I have my defects. After all, I am not strong to begin with, and I believe even Hercules fainted once. I attempt all day, at work, not to think about what lies ahead, but this costs me so much effort that there is nothing left for my work. I handle telephone calls so badly that after a while the switchboard operator refuses to connect me. So I had better say to myself, Go ahead and polish the silverware beautifully, then lay it out ready on the sideboard and be done with it. Because I polish it in my mind all day long—this is what torments me (and doesn't clean the silver).

I love German potato salad made with good, old potatoes and vinegar, even though it is so heavy, so coercive, almost, that I feel a little nauseated even before I taste it—I might be embracing an oppressive and alien culture. If I offer this to Milena I may be exposing a gross part of myself to her that I should spare her above all, a part of myself that she has not yet encountered. A French dish, however, even if more agreeable, would be less true to myself, and perhaps this would be an unpardonable betrayal.

I am full of good intentions and yet inactive, just as I was that day last summer when I sat on my balcony watching a beetle on its back waving its legs in the air, unable to right itself. I felt great sympathy for it, yet I would not leave my chair to help it. It stopped moving and was still for so long I thought it had died. Then a lizard walked over it, slid off it, and tipped it upright, and it ran up the wall as though nothing had happened.

I bought the tablecloth on the street yesterday from a man with a cart. The man was small, almost tiny, weak, and bearded, with one eye. I borrowed the candlesticks from a neighbor, or I should say, she lent them to me.

I will offer her espresso after dinner. As I plan this meal I feel a little the way Napoleon would have felt while designing the Russian campaign, if he had known exactly what the outcome would be.

I long to be with Milena, not just now but all the time. Why am I a human being? I ask myself—what an extremely vague condition! Why can't I be the happy wardrobe in her room?

Before I knew my dear Milena, I thought life itself was unbearable. Then she came into my life and showed me that that was not so. True, our first meeting was not auspicious, for her mother answered the door, and what a strong forehead the woman had, with an inscription on it which read: "I am dead, and I despise anyone who is not." Milena seemed pleased that I had come, but much more pleased when I left. That day, I happened to look at a map of the city. For a moment it seemed incomprehensible to me that anyone would build a whole city when all that is needed was a room for her.

Perhaps, in the end, the simplest thing would be to make for her exactly what I made for Felice, but with more care, so that nothing goes wrong, and without the snails or the mushrooms. I could even include the sauerbraten, though when I cooked it for Felice, I was still eating meat. At that time I was not bothered by the thought that an animal, too, has a right to a good life and perhaps even more important a good death. Now I can't even eat snails. My father's father was

12

a butcher and I vowed that the same quantity of meat he butchered in his lifetime was the quantity I would not eat in my own lifetime. For a long time now I have not tasted meat, though I eat milk and butter, but for Milena, I would make sauerbraten again.

My own appetite is never large. I am thinner than I should be, but I have been thin for a long time. Some years ago, for instance, I often went rowing on the Moldau in a small boat. I would row upriver and then lie on my back in the bottom of the boat and drift back down with the current. A friend once happened to be crossing a bridge and saw me floating along under it. He said it was as if Judgment Day had arrived and my coffin had been opened. But then he himself had grown almost fat by then, massive, and knew little about thin people except that they were thin. At least this weight on my feet is really my own property.

She may not even want to come anymore, not because she is fickle, but because she is exhausted, which is understandable. If she does not come it would be wrong to say I will miss her, because she is always so present in my imagination. Yet she will be at a different address and I will be sitting at the kitchen table with my face in my hands.

If she comes, I will smile and smile, I have inherited this from an old aunt of mine who also used to smile incessantly, but both of us out of embarrassment rather than good humor or compassion. I won't be able to speak, I won't even be happy, because after the preparation of the meal I won't have the strength. And if, with my sorry excuse for a first course resting in a bowl in my hands, I hesitate to leave the kitchen and enter the dining room, and if she, at the same time, feeling my embarrassment, hesitates to leave the living room and enter the dining room from the other side, then for that long interval the beautiful room will be empty.

Ah, well—one man fights at Marathon, the other in the kitchen.

Still, I have decided on nearly all the menu now and I have begun to prepare it by imagining our dinner, every detail of it, from beginning to end. I repeat this sentence to myself senselessly, my teeth chattering: "Then we'll run into the forest." Senselessly, because there is no forest here, and there would be no question of running in any case.

I have faith that she will come, though along with my faith is the same fear that always accompanies my faith, the fear that has been inherent in all faith, anyway, since the beginning of time.

Felice and I were not engaged at the time of that unfortunate dinner, though we had been engaged three years before and were to be engaged again one week later—surely not as a result of the dinner, unless Felice's compassion for me was further aroused by the futility of my efforts to make a good kasha varnishke, potato pancakes, and sauerbraten. Our eventual breakup, on the other hand, probably has more explanations than it really needs—this is ridiculous, but certain experts maintain that even the air here in this city may encourage inconstancy.

I was excited as one always is by something new. I was naturally somewhat frightened as well. I thought a traditional German or Czech meal might be best, even if rather heavy for July. I remained for some time undecided even in my dreams. At one point I simply gave up and contemplated leaving the city. Then I decided to stay, although simply lying around on the balcony may not really deserve to be called a decision. At these times I appear to be paralyzed with indecision while my thoughts are beating furiously within my head, just as a dragonfly appears to hang motionless in midair while its wings are beating furiously against the steady breeze. At last I jumped up like a stranger pulling another stranger out of bed.

The fact that I planned the meal carefully was probably insignificant. I wanted to prepare something wholesome, since she needed to build up her strength. I remember gathering the mushrooms in the early morning, creeping among the trees in plain sight of two elderly sisters—who appeared to disapprove deeply of me or my basket. Or perhaps of the fact that I was wearing a good suit in the forest. But their approval would have been more or less the same thing.

As the hour approached, I was afraid, for a little while, that she would not come, instead of being afraid, as I should have been, that she would in fact come. At first she had said she might not come. It was strange of her to do that. I was like an errand boy who could no longer run errands but still hoped for some kind of employment.

Just as a very small animal in the woods makes a disproportionate amount of noise and disturbance among the leaves and twigs on the ground when it is frightened and rushes to its hole, or even when it is not frightened but merely hunting for nuts, so that one thinks a bear is about to burst into the clearing, whereas it is only a mouse— this is what my emotion was like, so small and yet so noisy. I asked her please not to come to dinner, but then I asked her please not to listen to me but to come anyway. Our words are so often those of some unknown, alien being. I don't believe any speeches anymore. Even the most beautiful speech contains a worm.

Once, when we ate together in a restaurant, I was as ashamed of the dinner as though I had made it myself. The very first thing they brought to the table ruined our appetite for the rest, even if it had been any good: fat white *Leberknödeln* floating in a thin broth whose surface was dotted with oil. The dish was clearly German, rather than Czech. But why should anything be more complicated between us than if we were to sit quietly in a park and watch a hummingbird fly up from the petunias to rest at the top of a birch tree?

The night of our dinner, I told myself that if she did not come, I would enjoy the empty apartment, for if being alone in a room is necessary for life itself, being alone in an apartment is necessary if one is to be happy. I had borrowed the apartment for the occasion. But I had not been enjoying the happiness of the empty apartment. Or perhaps it wasn't the empty apartment that should have made me happy, but having two apartments. She did come, but she was late. She told me she had been delayed because she had had to wait to speak to a man who had himself been waiting, impatiently, for the outcome of a discussion concerning the opening of a new cabaret. I did not believe her.

When she walked in the door I was almost disappointed. She would have been so much happier dining with another man. She was going to bring me a flower, but appeared without it. Yet I was filled with such elation just to be with her, because of her love, and her kindness, as bright as the buzzing of a fly on a lime twig.

Despite our discomfort we proceeded with our dinner. As I gazed at the finished dish I lamented my waning strength, I lamented being born, I lamented the light of the sun. We ate something which unfortunately would not disappear from our plates unless we swallowed it. I was both moved and ashamed, happy and sad, that she ate with apparent enjoyment—ashamed and sad only that I did not have something better to offer her, moved and happy that it appeared to be enough, at least on this one occasion. It was only the grace with which she ate each part of the meal and the delicacy of her compliments that gave it any value—it was abysmally bad. She really deserved, instead, something like a baked sole or a breast of pheasant, with water ice and fruit from Spain. Couldn't I have provided this, somehow?

And when her compliments faltered, the language itself became pliant just for her, and more beautiful than one had any right to expect. If an uninformed stranger had heard Felice he would have thought, What a man! He must have moved mountains!—whereas I did almost nothing but mix the kasha as instructed by Ottla. I hoped that after she went away she would find a cool place like a garden in which to lie down on a deck chair and rest. As for myself, this pitcher was broken long before it went to the well.

There was the accident, too. I realized I was kneeling only when I saw her feet directly in front of my eyes. Snails were everywhere on the carpet, and the smell of garlic.

Perhaps, even so, once the meal was behind us, we did arithmetic tricks at the table, I don't remember, short sums, and then long sums while I gazed out the window at the building opposite. Perhaps we would have played music together instead, but I am not musical.

Our conversation was halting and awkward. I kept digressing senselessly, out of nervousness. Finally I told her I was losing my way, but it didn't matter because if she had come that far with me then we were both lost. There were so many misunderstandings, even when I did stay on the subject. And yet she shouldn't have been afraid that I was angry at her, but the opposite, that I wasn't.

She thought I had an Aunt Klara. It is true that I have an Aunt Klara, every Jew has an Aunt Klara. But mine died long ago. She said her own was quite peculiar, and inclined to make pronouncements, such as that one should stamp one's letters properly and not throw things out the window, both of which are true, of course, but not easy. We talked about the Germans. She hates the Germans so much, but I told her she shouldn't, because the Germans are wonderful. Perhaps my mistake was to boast that I had recently chopped wood for over an hour. I thought she should be grateful to me—after all, I was overcoming the temptation to say something unkind.

One more misunderstanding and she was ready to leave. We tried different ways of saying what we meant, but we weren't really lovers at that moment, just grammarians. Even animals, when they're quarreling, lose all caution: squirrels race back and forth across a lawn or a road and forget that there may be predators watching. I told her that if she were to leave, the only thing I would like about it would

17

be the kiss before she left. She assured me that although we were parting in anger, it would not be long before we saw each other again, but to my mind "sooner" rather than "never" was still just "never." Then she left.

With that loss I was more in the situation of Robinson Crusoe even than Robinson Crusoe himself—he at least still had the island, Friday, his supplies, his goats, the ship that took him away, his name. But as for me, I imagined some doctor with carbolic fingers taking my head between his knees and stuffing meat into my mouth and down my throat until I choked.

The evening was over. A goddess had walked out of the movie theater and a small porter was left standing by the tracks—and that was our dinner? I am so filthy—this is why I am always screaming about purity. No one sings as purely as those who inhabit the deepest hell—you think you're hearing the song of angels but it is that other song. Yet I decided to keep on living a little while longer, at least through the night.

After all, I am not graceful. Someone once said that I swim like a swan, but it was not a compliment.

Tropical Storm

Like a tropical storm,
I, too, may one day become "better organized."

Good Times

What was happening to them was that every bad time produced a bad feeling that in turn produced several more bad times and several more bad feelings, so that their life together became crowded with bad times and bad feelings, so crowded that almost nothing else could grow in that dark field. But then she had a feeling of peace one morning that lingered from the evening before spent sewing while he sat reading in the next room. And a day or two later, she had a feeling of contentment that lingered in the morning from the evening before when he kept her company in the kitchen while she washed the dinner dishes. If the good times increased, she thought, each good time might produce a good feeling that would in turn produce several more good times that would produce several more good feelings. What she meant was that the good times might multiply perhaps as rapidly as the square of the square, or perhaps more rapidly, like mice, or like mushrooms springing up overnight from the scattered spore of a parent mushroom which in turn had sprung up overnight with a crowd of others from the scattered spore of a parent, until her life with him would be so crowded with good times that the good times might crowd out the bad as the bad times had by now almost crowded out the good.

Idea for a Short
Documentary Film

Representatives of different food products manufacturers
try to open their own packaging.

Forbidden Subjects

Soon almost every subject they might want to talk about is associated with yet another unpleasant scene and becomes a subject they can't talk about, so that as time goes by there is less and less they can safely talk about, and eventually little else but the news and what they're reading, though not all of what they're reading. They can't talk about certain members of her family, his working hours, her working hours, rabbits, mice, dogs, certain foods, certain universities, hot weather, hot and cold room temperatures at night and in the day, lights on and lights off in the evening in summer, the piano, music in general, how much money he earns, what she earns, what she spends, etc. But one day, after they have been talking about a forbidden subject, though not the most dangerous of the forbidden subjects, she realizes it may be possible, sometimes, to say something calm and careful about a forbidden subject, so that it may once again become a subject that can be talked about, and then to say something calm and careful about another forbidden subject, so that there will be another subject that can be talked about once again, and that as more subjects can be talked about once again there will be, gradually, more talk between them, and that as there is more talk there will be more trust, and that when there is enough trust, they may dare to approach even the most dangerous of the forbidden subjects.

Two Types

Excitable

A woman was depressed and distraught for days after losing her pen.

Then she became so excited about an ad for a shoe sale that she drove three hours to a shoe store in Chicago.

Phlegmatic

A man spotted a fire in a dormitory one evening, and walked away to look for an extinguisher in another building. He found the extinguisher, and walked back to the fire with it.

The Senses

Many people treat their five senses with a certain respect and consideration. They take their eyes to a museum, their nose to a flower show, their hands to a fabric store for the velvet and silk; they surprise their ears with a concert, and excite their mouth with a restaurant meal.

But most people make their senses work hard for them day after day: Read me this newspaper! Pay attention, nose, in case the food is burning! Ears!—get together now and listen for a knock at the door!

Their senses have jobs to do and they do them, mostly—the ears of the deaf won't, and the eyes of the blind won't.

The senses get tired. Sometimes, long before the end, they say, I'm quitting—I'm getting out of this *now*.

And then the person is less prepared to meet the world, and stays at home more, without some of what he needs if he is to go on.

If it all quits on him, he is really alone: in the dark, in silence, numb hands, nothing in his mouth, nothing in his nostrils. He asks himself, Did I treat them wrong? Didn't I show them a good time?

Grammar Questions

Now, during the time he is dying, can I say, "This is where he lives"?

If someone asks me, "Where does he live?" should I answer, "Well, right now he is not living, he is dying"?

If someone asks me, "Where does he live?" can I say, "He lives in Vernon Hall"? Or should I say, "He is dying in Vernon Hall"?

When he is dead, I will be able to say, in the past tense, "He lived in Vernon Hall." I will also be able to say, "He died in Vernon Hall."

When he is dead, everything to do with him will be in the past tense. Or rather, the sentence "He is dead" will be in the present tense, and also questions such as "Where are they taking him?" or "Where is he now?"

But then I won't know if the words "he" and "him" are correct, in the present tense. Is he, once he is dead, still "he," and if so, for how long is he still "he"?

People may say "the body" and then call it "it." I will not be able to say "the body" in relation to him because to me he is still not something you would call "the body."

People may say "his body," but that does not seem right either. It is not "his" body because he does not own it, if he is no longer active or capable of owning anything.

I don't know if there is a "he," even though people will say "He is dead." But it does seem correct to say "he is dead." This may be the last time he will still be "he" in the present tense. Or it will not be the last time, because I will also say, "He is lying in his coffin." I will not say, and no one will say, "It is lying in the coffin," or "It is lying in its coffin."

I will continue to say "my father" in relation to him, after he dies, but will I say it only in the past tense, or also in the present tense?

He will be put in a box, not a coffin. Then, when he is in that box, will I say, "That is my father in that box," or "That was my father in that box," or will I say, "That, in the box, was my father"?

I will still say "my father," but maybe I will say it only as long as he looks like my father, or approximately like my father. Then, when he is in the form of ashes, will I point to the ashes and say, "That is my father"? Or will I say, "That was my father"? Or "Those ashes were my father"? Or "Those ashes are what was my father"?

When I later visit the graveyard, will I point and say, "My father is buried there," or will I say, "My father's ashes are buried there"? But the ashes will not belong to my father, he will not own them. They will be "the ashes that were my father."

In the phrase "he is dying," the words "he is" with the present participle suggest that he is actively doing something. But he is not actively dying. The only thing he is still actively doing is breathing. He looks as if he is breathing on purpose, because he is working hard at it, and frowning slightly. He is working at it, but surely he has no choice. Sometimes his frown deepens for just an instant, as though something is hurting him, or as though he is concentrating harder. Even though I can guess that he is frowning because of some pain inside him, or some other change, he still looks as though he is puzzled, or dislikes or disapproves of something. I've seen this expression on his face often in my life, though never before combined with these half-open eyes and this open mouth.

"He is dying" sounds more active than "He will be dead soon." That is probably because of the word "be"—we can "be" something whether we choose to or not. Whether he likes it or not, he "will be" dead soon. He is not eating.

"He is not eating" sounds active, too. But it is not his choice. He is not conscious that he is not eating. He is not conscious at all. But "is not eating" sounds more correct for him than "is dying" because of the negative. "Is not" seems correct for him, at the moment anyway, because he looks as though he is refusing something, because he is frowning.

Hand

Beyond the hand holding this book that I'm reading, I see another hand lying idle and slightly out of focus—my extra hand.

The Caterpillar

I find a small caterpillar in my bed in the morning. There is no good window to throw him from and I don't crush or kill a living thing if I don't have to. I will go to the trouble of carrying this thin, dark, hairless little caterpillar down the stairs and out to the garden.

He is not an inchworm, though he is the size of an inchworm. He does not hump up in the middle but travels steadily along on his many pairs of legs. As I leave the bedroom, he is quite speedily walking around the slopes of my hand.

But halfway down the stairs, he is gone—my hand is blank on every side. The caterpillar must have let go and dropped. I can't see him. The stairwell is dim and the stairs are painted dark brown. I could get a flashlight and search for this tiny thing, in order to save his life. But I will not go that far—he will have to do the best he can. Yet how can he make his way down to the back door and out into the garden?

I go on about my business. I think I've forgotten him, but I haven't. Every time I go upstairs or down, I avoid his side of the stairs. I am sure he is there trying to get down.

At last I give in. I get the flashlight. Now the trouble is that the stairs are so dirty. I don't clean them because no one ever sees them here in the dark. And the caterpillar is, or was, so small. Many things under the beam of the flashlight look rather like him—a very slim splinter of wood or a thick piece of thread. But when I poke them, they don't move.

I look on every step on his side of the stairs, and then on both sides. You get somewhat attached to any living thing once you try to help it. But he is nowhere. There is so much dust and dog hair on the steps. The dust may have stuck to his little body and made it hard for him to move or at least to go in the direction he wanted to go in. It may have dried him out. But why would he even go down instead of up? I haven't looked on the landing above where he disappeared. I will not go that far.

I go back to my work. Then I begin to forget the caterpillar. I forget him for as long as one hour, until I happen to go to the stairs again. This time I see that there is something just the right size, shape, and color on one of the steps. But it is flat and dry. It can't have started out as him. It must be a short pine needle or some other plant part.

The next time I think of him, I see that I have forgotten him for several hours. I think of him only when I go up or down the stairs. After all, he is really there somewhere, trying to find his way to a green leaf, or dying. But already I don't care as much. Soon, I'm sure, I will forget him entirely.

Later there is an unpleasant animal smell lingering about the stairwell, but it can't be him. He is too small to have any smell. He has probably died by now. He is simply too small, really, for me to go on thinking about him.

Childcare

It's his turn to take care of the baby. He is cross.

He says, "I never get enough done."

The baby is in a bad mood, too.

He gives the baby a bottle of juice and sits him well back in a big armchair.

He sits himself down in another chair and turns on the television.

Together they watch *The Odd Couple*.

We Miss You: A Study of
Get-Well Letters from a Class
of Fourth-Graders

The following is a study of twenty-seven get-well letters written by a class of fourth-graders to their classmate Stephen, when he was in the hospital recovering from a serious case of osteomyelitis.

The disease set in after a rather mysterious accident involving a car. Young Stephen, according to his own later report and a brief notice in the local newspaper, was returning home by himself at dusk one day in early December. He stepped into the street, preparing to cross, and was hit obliquely by a slow-moving car, not with great force, but with enough force to knock him to the ground. The driver of the car, a man of indeterminate age, stopped and got out to see if the boy was all right. Ascertaining that no great harm had been done, the man drove on. In fact, the boy had hurt his knee but said nothing about the accident at home, out of embarrassment or a perception that he was somehow to blame. The knee, untreated, became infected; the osteomyelitis bacteria entering the wound; the boy became seriously ill and was hospitalized. After some weeks, and worry on the part of his doctors, family, and friends, he recovered, thanks in part to the recently developed drug penicillin, and was discharged.

At the time of Stephen's hospitalization, his parents put the following notice in the local paper in an attempt to locate the driver of the car. The notice was headlined PARENTS SEEK TO TALK TO DRIVER OF CAR IN ACCIDENT. It read:

About the first week of December, Stephen, son of Mr. and Mrs. B. of 94 N. Rd., at the corner of Elm and Crescent Streets in the late afternoon, was struck very lightly by a car whose driver got out and looked the boy over and discussed it with him. Then each went on his way.

The parents of the boy would like to get in touch with the driver of the vehicle and are appealing to him to communicate with them.

There was no response to the notice.

After the Christmas holidays were over and his classmates returned to school, the children's teacher, Miss F., assigned them to write Stephen a get-well letter. She then corrected the letters sparingly but precisely and sent them in a packet to Stephen. This was a school exercise clearly intended, if we may judge from the number of consistent features, to teach certain letter-writing skills.

The School

The school in which these letters were written was a large brick building dedicated to use by classes from kindergarten through eighth grade and situated in the heart of a pleasant residential neighborhood. The streets were lined with mature shade trees, and the

houses were for the most part roomy and comfortable but unostenta-
tious middle-class homes with modest or, occasionally, generous
yards planted with lawns and a variety of trees, shrubs, and flowers.
Most of the children lived in the immediate neighborhood of the
school and walked to and from school by themselves or with friends
on sidewalks that were well maintained but here and there cracked or
buckled by the roots of the large trees. Stephen himself, along with
his neighbors Carol and Jonathan, lived one street over from the
school. At the corner of the street on which the school stood was a
small store owned and presided over by a matronly woman with a
rather forbidding manner. It sold candy and a limited range of groceries, and was heavily patronized by the children after school.
Across from this store, a street descended steeply toward a broad,
shallow river in which the children were not allowed to swim because
of effluents from the factories upstream. The school building was
surrounded by a large asphalt playground lacking climbing or swinging equipment. The classrooms were well lighted, with natural day-
light coming in through large windows.

General Appearance and Form of the Letters

The letters are written on lined exercise paper of two different sizes,
most of them on the smaller, 7″ by 8 ½″, four of them on the larger,
8″ by 10 ½″. Although the paper is of a low grade and was manufac-
tured nearly sixty years ago, it has remained supple and smooth in
texture, and the letters are still clearly legible, some students in particular having borne down heavily to make very dark and distinct
lines. They are all written in ink, though the ink varies, some blue and
some black, some dark and some light, some lines thin and some thick.

The penmanship is for the most part quite good, i.e., the script
slopes at a fairly consistent angle to the right, most letters touch the
line, the letters are evenly spaced, the uprights of the letters do not
touch the line above, etc., though the variations in thickness of line

and formation of letters, as well as the wavering lines, betray the tremulous hands and labored efforts of the novice script-users. Some of the capitals, however, are very elegantly formed, with a handsome flourish.

There are twenty-seven letters altogether, written by thirteen girls and fourteen boys. Twenty-four of the children's letters are dated January 4, evidently the day on which the teacher set them to work as a group; two are dated January 5, and one January 8, implying that these children were absent on the day the exercise was initiated.

The letters all carry the same heading, obviously prescribed by the teacher, on three lines in the upper-right-hand corner: the name of the school; the town and state; and the date. They are ruled by hand in pencil down the left margin to provide a uniform indented guide for the beginning of each line, with the exception of the January 8 letter—this latecomer evidently was not given the instruction or did not hear it—and those written on the larger sheets of paper, which bear a printed rule down the left margin. The hand-ruled lines vary: some are thin and straight, others thick and slanted, and one trails off at an angle at the bottom, the pupil having evidently reached the end of his ruler before he reached the bottom of the page.

The salutations are all the same: "Dear Stephen." The closings vary within a narrow range: "Your friend" (5 boys and 10 girls); "Your classmate" (3 girls and 2 boys); "Your pal" (4 boys); "Sincerely yours" (1 boy); "Love" (1 boy); and "Your pal of pals" (1 boy: this was Jonathan, a close friend). It should be noted that only the boys use the colloquial "pal," whereas nearly twice as many girls as boys use the more formal "friend."

The teacher has inked in corrections on some of the letters, in the darkest ink and a smaller hand. She has added commas where missing (most frequently after the salutation, "Dear Stephen," the closing, e.g. "Your friend," and between the name of the town and the state) and question marks where required. She has corrected some misspellings ("happey," "sleding," "throught," "brouther," and "We are mississ you very much"). In one case she has, surprisingly, had to correct the spelling of a child's name, reducing "Arilene" to "Arlene." She has supplied two missing words. Several errors have escaped her notice. On the whole, the letters are spelled and punctuated correctly; the teacher makes, on average, only about one correction per page, and most of these are punctuation corrections. Either the students have learned their lessons very well or, perhaps more likely, these are fair copies of rough, corrected drafts.

Twenty-two children sign their full names, first and last. One signs "Billy J." and the remaining four sign only their first names. (For reasons of confidentiality, only the initial letter of the children's last names will be retained here.)

LENGTH

Excluding the salutation and closing, the letters range in length from three to eight lines and from two to eight sentences. None of the boys' letters is longer than five sentences, whereas, of the girls, one each has a letter containing six, seven, and eight sentences. Although the girls number one fewer than the boys, they are overall more communicative, contributing 84 lines versus the boys' 66, and 61 sentences versus the boys' 53.

Not all of the girls, however, are communicative. Two write letters containing only three lines and three sentences. One is the gloomy letter by Sally quoted below. The second brief letter, by Susan B., includes what may be an envious reference to a box of candy. In general, the length and content of the shortest letters appear to connote depressive or apathetic states of mind in their authors, while the content and length of the longest give the impression of being the products of the more cheerful and outgoing temperaments. Those in the mid-length range variously express stout realism (broken branches and fallen snowmen), bland formulae (see

Maureen's letter below), or strong feelings and personality (Scott's "I'd yank you out of bed").

OVERALL COHERENCE

There is a tendency toward non-sequiturs in the letters: one sentence often has little to do with the sentence that follows or precedes it (e.g., "The temperature keeps on changing. I can't wait until you come back to school").

Some letters, however, develop one idea with perfect cogency throughout: e.g., Sally's grim letter, Scott's enthusiastic, somewhat violent letter threatening to "yank" Stephen out of bed, and Alex's informative letter about sledding, which names the location of the sledding and notes progress from last year: "We had some fun over at Hospital Hill. We went over a big bump and went flying through the air. This year I went on a higher part than I used to."

SENTENCE STRUCTURES

The letters overall contain a predominance of simple sentences (e.g., "There was a big snowball fight outside"), with now and then a compound, complex, or compound-complex sentence.

COMPOUND SENTENCES

The shortest letter (two sentences) is written by Peter. He is the same boy whose ruled line is thick, slanted, and bent at the bottom. However, he is also one of the few students to form a compound sentence, and in so doing uses the rarer and more interesting conjunction *but*: "We are having a very happy time but we miss you."

Another who uses *but* is Cynthia, one of the realists in the class: "I have made snowmen but they have fallen down."

Susan A., another realist, uses *but* to modify her description of fairyland, as quoted below.

Other conjunctions used in the letters are: *until* (2), *because* (2), and the most common and inexpressive or neutral: *and* (7).

One girl, Carol, using the conjunction *because*, forms two compound sentences in a letter which is only three sentences long: "I hope you will be back to school very soon because it is lonesome without you" and "New Year's Eve your [little] Sister slept at our house because your Mother and Father and [older] Sister went to a party." Because she employs more elaborate sentence structures, her letter is one of those containing the most lines (8) yet the fewest sentences (3).

The most common, and least expressive, conjunction is *and* (7 occurrences), as in Alex's sentence: "We went over a big bump and went flying through the air." One girl, Diane, forms a compound sentence out of two imperatives: "Hurry up and come back."

COMPLEX SENTENCES

Aside from the frequent formulaic complex sentences beginning with "I hope" (e.g., "I hope you get better") and "I wish" (e.g., "I wish you saw it"), there are relatively few instances of complex sentences:

Fred: "Well I guess this is all I have to tell you."

Theodore: "I beat the boys who were against me."

Alex: "This year I went on a higher part than I used to."

Susan B.: "Jonathan A. told me that he send [*sic*] you a big box of candy."

Kingsley has two complex sentences in succession: "What do you think you are going to get for Christmas?" and "I got every thing I wanted to get."

COMPOUND-COMPLEX SENTENCES

Van, the boy who admits to being uninspired and writes one of the briefest letters, is also, however, one of the few pupils to construct a compound-complex sentence, though he omits two words and contradicts himself (see his use of *think*): "I think that is all to say [*sic*] because I just can't think."

Jonathan also constructs a compound-complex sentence. His is more cheerful but uses a less expressive conjunction: "I hope you liked my box of candy, and I can hardly wait until you will be home again."

Susan A. uses the more loaded conjunction *but*: "When it was over everything looked like a fairyland but some trees were bent and broken." She follows this sentence with another compound-complex sentence, using the strong conjunction *so* and including an imperative: "We are very sorry that you are in the hospital, so get well quick."

VERBS

Some of the children's verb tenses are unclear.

Apropos a movie, Theodore writes: "I wish you saw it." It is unclear whether he means "I wish you could see it" or "I wish you had seen it."

Billy T. writes: "I hope you will eat well." It is not clear when or where Stephen should eat well.

Joseph A. writes: "I hope you have fun." It is not clear when or where Stephen should have fun. Both Billy and Joseph probably intended the meaning conveyed by the present participle forms "are eating well" and "are having fun." It may be noted that Joseph is the only child to associate Stephen's stay in the hospital with having fun.

The most vivid verb is Scott's Anglo-Saxon *yank*.

IMPERATIVES

The only instances of use of the imperative (4, one softened by "Please") are found in the letters of girls. This may imply a greater inclination to "command" or "boss" on the part of the girls than the boys, but may also be statistically insignificant, given the small number of letters in the sample.

STYLE

The style of the letters is for the most part informal, i.e., neither excessively formal nor extremely casual or colloquial. Occasionally, the diction becomes conversational: there are two instances of *Well* as openings of sentences (both omit the comma that should follow). There is a vivid conversational verb, *yank*, in Scott's letter. It is worth noting, however, a conspicuous formality common to most of the children on at least one point: given a choice, as they seem to have been, most of the children sign their full names to their letters. Also, in the two instances in which children refer to other children by name, they use the full name, even though Stephen would have known perfectly well from the context which child they were talking about. It may be that in the school setting, first and last names were so commonly used inseparably by the teacher in calling the roll or in reprimanding, that when writing in school, in any case, the children profoundly identified each other and themselves by first and last names both.

Two of the children achieve moments of stylistic eloquence. One, Susan A., creates a vivid concrete image which is enhanced by her use of alliteration and a forceful rhythm: "some trees were bent and broken." The other, Sally, opens with a powerful specific image—"Your seat is empty"—and then reinforces it with parallel structure: "Your stocking is not finished."

It could be argued that Scott, too, achieves a certain pleasing balance with his alternation, in the four sentences of his cogent letter, between "over there" and "here where we are," "up there" and "back here again," in fact creating a seesaw motion and thereby tying Stephen more closely to the class than any of the other children.

CONTENT

Some of the letters are bland and/or inexpressive, while others are more informative and more colorful, and/or express their writers' personalities more vividly.

Probably the blandest letter, in that it includes all the most commonly expressed formulaic sentiments and only the most general "news," with no departures from convention in content or style that would express an individual personality, is Maureen's. Although it is undeniably friendly and cheerful, the friendliness and cheerfulness seem somewhat rote: "How are you feeling? I miss you very much. I hope that you will be back in school soon. I like school very much. I had a very nice time in the snow." Her handwriting is round and slants consistently to the right with one notable exception: the word *I*, which is vertical. It may not be going too far to suggest that these markedly contrasting *I*'s express a sublimated rebelliousness, a suppressed desire to be less conformist and obedient than she evidently is.

Another fairly bland letter, in a small, round script, is Mary's, although she is slightly more emphatic than Maureen—"We all miss you very much"—and adds one specific: "I have had lots of fun playing with my sled in the snow."

The content can be generally summarized as falling under the following headings, within the two more general categories of expressions of sympathy and "news":

Formulaic Expressions of Sympathy
come back soon/wish you were here
    (17 occurrences in 27 letters)
how are you/hope you are feeling better (16)
miss you (9)
experience in hospital/food (4)
empathy: I know how it feels (2)

News
playing in snow (9)
Christmas/Christmas presents (7)
school/schoolwork (4)
eating/food (4)
weather (3)
shopping with parent (2)

movies (2)

pets (1)

New Year's Eve (1)

Stephen's family (1)

party (1)

FORMULAIC EXPRESSIONS OF SYMPATHY

Miss You

Many of the children's letters include the standard "We [or I] miss you" or "We [or I] miss you very much," often paired with "We [or I] hope you will be back soon."

Van opens with those two sentiments and then finds himself at a loss: in thin, tremulous handwriting, with so little space between the words that they almost touch, he closes with "I think that is all to say [*sic*] because I just can't think." Some of Van's letters sit nicely on the line, some float up above it, and some sink below it. It is possible, in his case—as in others in which the child betrays some anxiety—that the letters do not sit on the line because the child is overcompensating: for fear of letting his letters sink below the line, he keeps them up off the line; for fear of letting them float up off the line, he forces them down below it. We must remember, when imagining these children learning to write neat script, that a line is not an actual resting place for a letter. It is a conceptual mark, and a very thin one, and a beginning writer finds it difficult to touch that line exactly with each letter. There is thus a certain amount of anxiety, for some children, even in the act of writing script, regardless of what they are trying to express.

Joan is more specific, and thus more poignant, immediately evoking the classroom: "I miss you in our row in school." She conveys, in addition, a sense of solidarity among the children in that particular row—"our row."

Sally is even more specific, and her letter, though one of the briefest, carries the most powerful, and the darkest, emotional burden: "Hope you are feeling better. Your seat is empty. Your stocking is not finished." This last sentence is followed by a period, but then, ambiguously, by a lower-case *b*, so that we cannot be sure whether Sally meant to continue the sentence or begin a new one when she goes on to say, again dwelling on darker possibilities: "but I don't think it will be finished." The function of the *but* is also unclear. Sally's handwriting is faint and thin, and the letters extremely small, except when, as she has evidently mistaken the teacher's instructions, the tall letters such as *f* and *l* extend hesitantly all the way up to touch the line above. The content, along with the brevity of the letter and Sally's small handwriting, would seem to indicate either an innate pessimism or a low self-esteem, despite the quite exceptional exuberance and panache of her capital *H*.

How Are You/Hope You Are Feeling Better
Another commonly expressed sentiment is: "We [or I] hope you are feeling well/will feel better soon/will get well soon/how are you feeling?"

Billy J. opens with "I hope you are feeling well," closes with "I hope you will be back soon," and adds only one sentence in between: "We are not doing much." The words "not doing much" are smaller and more compact than the rest, perhaps reflecting the content of the remark. Billy's letters also tend to sink below the line, according well in spirit with his only news—that not much is being accomplished.

Lois strikes a conversational note that is stylistically unusual among the letters when she writes, in bold black script that sits squarely on the line but sometimes disappears off the right side of the page: "How are you feeling now? Better, I hope."

Joseph A., instead of writing "How are you?," writes "How do you?" The teacher does not notice this.

45

Lois, who manages eight sentences within the space of her six lines, expresses this sentiment twice, once at the beginning—"When will you be back?"—and once, employing a courteous command, at the end—"Please try to come back soon."

Carol's letter, as quoted above, adds the intensifying explanation "because it is lonesome without you"—either quite sincere, since she lives next door to Stephen and may be a close friend, or at least polite. It should be noted that Carol stands in a privileged relationship to Stephen, since their families are also friends, as her letter clearly indicates.

The enthusiastic Joseph goes further, expressing impatience: "I can't wait until you come back to school."

Stephen's friend Jonathan, whose handwriting is well-rounded and upright, each letter sitting firmly on the line, uses almost the same words: "I can hardly wait until you will be home again." Presumably, Jonathan replaces the more common "back to school" with "home again" because he is not only a good friend but a neighbor.

One girl, Diane, expresses the same sentiment in almost the same words—"I can hardly wait for you to come back to school"—and then reinforces it with a second sentence that employs two imperatives: "Hurry up and come back."

Her friend Mary K. expresses it more precisely and rather severely, hoping that Stephen "will be back in school in a very short time."

Billy T. emphasizes Stephen's discharge from the hospital rather than his return to school. He also devotes two of the three sentences of his brief letter to this idea: "When will you be out? I hope you will be out soon."

Another boy, Scott, expresses this sentiment in one of the most cogent letters, in which each sentence follows logically from the one preceding. He begins with empathy: "I know how it feels over there," and then develops his idea, first repeating his expression of empathy (unusual among the letters): "I think you would like to be here where we are." Now he adds a note of drama, along with a rare use of the subjunctive: "And if I were up there I'd yank you out of bed." Finally he completes his back-and-forth structure with another reference to the school and the logical—"Then"—result of his imagined action: "Then you could be back here again." (Scott's phrases "over there" and "up there" signal his awareness that the hospital is some distance from the town and on an elevated site, a fact supported by Jonathan's identical use of "up there" and a third child's reference to "Hospital Hill" in a description of sledding.)

One girl, Susan B., in one of the briefer letters (three lines, three sentences), expresses only the common sentiments and then adds the wistful secondhand report: "Jonathan A. told me that he send [*sic*] you a big box of candy." Her handwriting changes noticeably in the latter part of this sentence: dark, upright, and confident at the start of her letter, the words become increasingly faint and slant more and more to the right until the word *candy*, thin and delicate, is lying almost on its side.

Experience in Hospital/Food

Only a few children express curiosity about Stephen's experience in the hospital.

Kingsley asks: "Do you like it at the hospital?"

Stephen's good friend Jonathan, too, is interested: "How is it up there?"

Stephen's next-door neighbor, Carol, is more specific: "Do you have good meals there?"

Billy T. is also concerned about Stephen's food, presumably in the hospital, although his use of the future tense makes this somewhat unclear: "I hope you will eat well."

Arlene, who was evidently not sure how to spell her own name, or perhaps chose to decorate it with the added *i*, brings a tone of urgency or even peremptoriness to her letter, with her two brief but exact questions: "Who is your nurse? Who is your doctor?" We understand, however, when we come to the last sentence in her letter, that her interest may be "professional": "I got a nurse kit for Christmas."

Empathy: I Know How It Feels

Scott opens with a display of empathy—"I know how it feels over there"—before threatening to visit Stephen.

Joseph O. also opens with what seems to be generous empathy: "I know how you feel." But he then continues with an apparent non-sequitur: "I am going to get a new coat with a hood."

NEWS

Weather

A few children mention the weather.

Joseph A. says, laconically or reasonably: "The temperature keeps on changing."

Cynthia, who has a good understanding of the importance of accuracy and detail (see below), writes: "It's very icey [sic] out today."

Another girl, Susan A., is more poetical about the weather, deploying the only metaphor in the entire sample of letters. Although the metaphor is a hackneyed one, she immediately afterward improves on it with a more powerful realistic description: "A week ago we had a sleet storm. When it was over everything looked like a fairyland but some trees were bent and broken." Her ultimately matter-of-fact and realistic approach to her surroundings is reflected in handwriting that is quite regular, except for some tremulous lines in the taller letters.

Eating / Food

Aside from the two mentions of eating in relation to Stephen's hospital experience, the only mentions of food are the two references to

Jonathan's gift of the box of candy, one by Jonathan himself ("I hope you liked my box of candy") and the other by the perhaps envious Susan B.

School/Schoolwork

Aside from the commonly expressed wish that Stephen would return to school soon, school and schoolwork are not mentioned by many of the students, perhaps because they are sitting in school as they write.

Diane is the only student to mention a textbook: "We are reading in Singing Wheels." We may even posit, on the basis of her exceptional interest in this text, along with her subsequent mention of receiving a Victrola for Christmas, implying an interest in music, together with her inconsistent handwriting (letters sometimes slanted and sometimes upright, sometimes sinking below the line, etc.), that Diane is rather intellectually and artistically inclined, and "creative." At the same time, given her inclusion of her siblings in her letter (see below), as well as her friendship with Mary, and Mary's mention of their skiing, she appears to be outgoing, sociable, family-oriented, and physically active.

The above-mentioned friend, Mary K., after she describes skiing with Diane, closes her letter: "Well we are starting reading now so I will have to say, 'Good-by.' " (The teacher, although she inserted the hyphen in "Good-by," has not supplied the missing comma after "Well.") Mary is the only one to evoke the classroom at the moment the children are writing, by mentioning an imminent classroom activity. She evidently shares Diane's interest in, or enjoyment of, the class's activity of reading.

A third mention of school, but in the most general terms, is the bland remark by Maureen quoted earlier: "I like school very much." As we observed earlier, however, Maureen may not like school as much as she says she does.

A fourth girl, Lois, mentions another area of study, perhaps one that interests her more than reading: "We are still on tables." She precedes this, however, by the disclaimer: "We are not doing very much work." (It should be pointed out that despite the evident care with which the teacher has conducted this exercise, two students comment that they are "not doing much/not doing very much work." This is either true or, more likely, merely the perception of these particular students, who may, if such is the case, be either brighter and quicker to finish their work than some of the others or simply less interested. Whatever the case, the teacher has allowed these remarks to stand.)

Shopping with Parent
The children go downtown to shop, they shop for winter clothes, and they go with their mothers.

Fred writes: "My Mother and I are going down town to get a stormcoat. My Sister is going to get a new skisuit and a hat." This is the entire content of the letter, aside from his closing sentence: "Well I guess this is all I have to tell you." (Again, the teacher has failed to supply the missing comma after "Well.")

Playing in Snow
The children are generally more expressive about their play in the snow than any other subject, sometimes providing place-names and other details.

Alex writes: "We had some fun over at Hospital Hill. We went over a big bump and went flying through the air. This year I went on a higher part than I used to." His handwriting, perhaps in keeping with his sense of adventure, is inconsistent, the letters sometimes on the line and sometimes above or below it, the ink laid down sometimes in a thin, elegant stroke, sometimes a thick, awkward one.

Two boys describe fights. John W. writes, "There was a big snowball fight outside. Almost all of the groups were fighting." Since any snowball fight would necessarily take place outside, his use of "outside" must be local and specific, indicating the school grounds, especially since only there would "almost all of the groups" be present. Stephen was evidently expected to know exactly who constituted "all of the groups."

Theodore writes: "I had a snowball fight with some boys down at my house. I beat the boys who were against me."

The realist Cynthia, not as combative as the boys, writes in firm dark ink, "I have been sliding once and I had fun. I have made snowmen but they have fallen down." The consistent slope of her letters, her sensitive use of parallel structure, and her precision as to the frequency and results of her activities suggest that she may be a good student.

Mary K. is one of only two to mention another child by name: "Last Monday Diane T. and I went skiing. There is a small jump in the hill and we had a hard time jumping it." Her somewhat stern "I hope you . . . will be back in school in a very short time," in addition to the specificity of "small jump" and "hard time" may lead us to posit that she demands a fairly high standard of performance from herself as well as from others.

Janet adds an unexpected element: "I have been sledding and skiing and the cats go with me." This may be one of the few instances, among the letters, of objectively interesting information. Before signing off, she notes, less interestingly, "They sleep with me, too."

Lois's reference to the snow is general, and therefore less interesting, but she is the only one, kindly, to include mention of Stephen in the activity: "Sorry you can't be with us in the snow."

Movies
Stephen is also included in Theodore's report of going to the movies: "A few days ago I went to see Marine Raiders and Stagecoach Kid. I wish you saw it."

John C. also writes about going to the movies and names not only the movies but the town, though his use of *And* is unclear: "I went to P. [a nearby town]. And I went to the movies once in P. I saw Branded." His script is gracefully formed but unusually consistent in sinking down slightly below the line. This may indicate a desire for more stability on his part, a fear of imagination, or, on the contrary, an unusually firmly grounded personality. His mention of the movie, however, may allow us to posit that he is attracted to works of the imagination, but at the same time reacts against their inherently unsettling presentation of an alternate reality by attempting to ground himself more firmly in his own reality.

It is notable that whereas the children are not always specific about other subjects in their letters, they take pains to supply the titles of the movies they have seen.

Christmas / Christmas Presents

Some of the children list their Christmas presents without comment. Others offer a general comment without specifying what they received.

Diane includes her siblings' presents, too: "I got a victrola for Christmas. My sister got a doll carriage. My brother got a football." It is unclear whether these were their only presents, or merely the most noteworthy.

John C., on the other hand, appears to be giving a complete list, and displays a nice sense of order in progressing from the greatest to the smallest number in his enumeration: "I got three cowboy books, two games, and a flashlight for Christmas."

Joan is not specific, but she mentions a sibling and introduces her sentence about Christmas presents with a general statement: "I had a nice Christmas. My brother and I have very nice Christmas presents."

Jonathan is one of three who ask about Stephen's presents: "Did you get alot of toys for Christmas?"

Janet is less interested in quantity and wants specifics: "What did you get for Christmas?" She follows up with a second question that could refer to both quality and quantity: "Was Santa good to you?"

Kingsley is the only one to assume, rightly or wrongly, that because Stephen is in the hospital, he has not yet celebrated Christmas: "What do you think you are going to get for Christmas?" In keeping, perhaps, with the tentative nature of his question, the word *think* rises off the line and then returns to it. He follows this question with a general statement of satisfaction: "I got every thing I wanted to get." Some of his letters are much larger than others, e.g., the *b* in *better* and the *C* in *Christmas*—both of which may have been especially significant words for this boy.

Conclusion: The Daily Lives of the Children, Their Awareness of Space and Time, and Their Characters and States of Mind

We may confidently form some idea of the children's daily lives, characters, and moods from these letters, as well as their perceptions of space and time, even though the letters may to some extent misrepresent the truth because of the circumstances under which they were written: the teacher may have limited their choices as to appropriate subjects, and was surely present at the front of the room overseeing the exercise; the children did not choose to write the letters, but were compelled to write them; they were also aware that they had only a limited amount of time in which to write them and that the next subject loomed ("Well we are starting reading now").

DAILY LIVES

If we are to believe most of the information contained in the letters, we may ascertain at least the following about the children: Their possessions are relatively few—in any case, they are satisfied with as few as five fairly modest Christmas presents (see John C.), although quantity is clearly of interest to them (see Jonathan). They spend time with family members and classmates. Their activities include playing in the snow (both sledding and skiing), going to the movies, shopping downtown, and occasionally traveling out of town. Some have pets and strong friendships, and some have an interest in school-work. Some of the boys are interested in cowboys, reading, football, and the movies; some of the girls in music, dolls, and nursing. Both boys and girls like to play outdoors.

TIME

In general, the children's sense of time and place is well developed. The letters overall contain a clear sense of the past (e.g., what they got for Christmas), the present ("Your seat is empty"), and the future ("My Sister is going to get a new skisuit"). Some of the children anticipate Stephen's return in the future. Only Jonathan promises further communication: "I will send you more letters soon."

The immediate future at the time of the writing is evoked, exceptionally, by Mary K. ("Well we are starting reading now").

PLACE

The letters also show that the children have a clear and accurate sense of where they are in space. As they sit in their schoolroom writing, they are in fact on a higher elevation than the center of town, which they not only colloquially but also correctly refer to as "down town." They are closer to the center of town, however, than is the hospital, which they locate "over there." Their plateau is also lower than the elevation on which the hospital sits, which they refer to as "up there." "Up there" may also indicate their awareness of the fact that the hospital lies slightly to the north of the town.

It may also be pertinent to suggest that in the phrase "over there" we see a rare coincidence of actual and psychological space, in that their use of the phrase quite possibly signals an attempt on their part to distance themselves firmly from the hospital and its implied threat of death and disease.

The immediate space of the classroom is evoked by Joan and by Susan B. with their respective references to "in our row" and "Your seat is empty."

It should be noted, in addition, that some children are more pre-occupied generally by the outdoors ("we went skiing") while some are more concerned with interior spaces (the classroom, row or seat; the hospital). There is also, besides the distancing "over there," a general, perhaps anxious, identification of the hospital with the direction "out" (Billy T.'s "When will you be out?") in contrast to the reassuring identification of the school with "in" and "back in" (Mary K.).

CHARACTERS AND STATES OF MIND

The teacher, though carefully controlling the form and general content of the letters, seems to have allowed the students to follow their own desires as to specific content and style, perhaps within certain limits. This being the case, the children's choices of subject matter, along with their treatment of it, may give us clues as to their different characters and temperaments.

Some children indicate a high degree of self-sufficiency, entertaining themselves (outdoor play), while others reveal some dependence on "packaged" or "ready-made" entertainment (two instances of trips to the movies). Some reveal more inclination toward activity in general, whether physical or cultural (outdoor play, movies), while others are more concerned with material acquisition (Christmas presents, shopping trips); and finally, a majority of the children focus on outer-directed or interactive activities of one kind or another (play, shopping), while a small percentage seem preoccupied by certain ideas or mental states (you are gone, your seat is empty, "I just can't think").

Some show an inclination toward an interactive social world outside the family ("Diane T. and I"), while others are oriented more toward a domestic or familial world (shopping with Mother). Including siblings in accounts of the Christmas holiday ("My sister got a doll carriage. My brother got a football") may reveal feelings of insecurity and a need to identify with the large family unit.

Some children display boldness ("I'd yank you out of bed"); or a quest for adventure ("This year I went on a higher part than I used to"); while others dwell on absence and lack ("I just can't think"; and the refrain of "I miss you" and "We miss you"). Some strike a sad note (Carol's "lonesome"; Sally's "Your seat is empty"); or hint at a feeling of failure and/or defeat (fallen snowman, bent and broken branches); or of jealousy/envy/deprivation (another child received the box of candy). Some are peremptory in their tone (the girls' use of the imperative) and some are loving (Janet's obvious fondness for her pets). Some of the children are more sensitive to difficulty and loneliness than others. But all the children are capable of expressing friendly feelings toward a classmate in an unfortunate situation, at least when they are assigned to do so.

Some of the children display contradictory traits or inner conflict, as noted in the case of Maureen above. Another case is that of Arlene: although she is eminently practical, and seems sincere in her choice of nursing as a profession, she may betray a degree of suppressed romanticism (and thus an attraction toward a less practical vocation) in her highly unusual alteration of her own name from the more down-to-earth "Arlene" to the prettier and more fanciful "Arilene."

Although the dominant mood expressed by the letters appears to be positive and optimistic, some of the children's choices of subject matter and style betray a certain fear or uneasiness, or an awareness of the darker side of their lives (snowball fight, difficulty with jump), and this generalized fear may be present in all the children to some extent (e.g., the anxious repetition of "I hope . . . I hope . . .").

In fact, although theirs would appear to have been a relatively safe world—including sledding, Christmas presents, shopping with Mother—it had its darker side: bent and broken branches, fallen snowmen, the empty seat and the unfinished stocking, the box of candy that went to another child. What did they feel as they played on Hospital Hill, with the hospital itself looming over them? Were they aware of Stephen, alone, perhaps looking out at them? Were they perhaps always half conscious that Stephen's sudden accident might equally well have happened to them? The children were, it should be kept in mind, already deeply familiar with an environment that was confusingly paradoxical and vaguely threatening: the outdoor fun of sledding and skiing could take place only within sight of the grim façade of the hospital above them; their after-school treats could be gained only through an encounter with the hostile proprietor of the corner store, and would then be unwrapped within sight of the steep drop toward the slow-moving but dangerous river. More generally, in fact, one might say that these children, caught between the implicit threat of the hospital on the hill and the more explicit threat of the river down below, may indeed have wished to slip away, as they often enough did, out of reach of both these menaces, toward "down town" with its offerings of tempting merchandise in Mother's company, or even out of town altogether (a trip to P.), or into the fictional world offered by the movie theaters, the cowboy books, and their own imaginations ("fairyland").

Addendum

Of interest, for comparison, may be a letter in Stephen's own handwriting, on an unlined page, written after he returned home, in which he thanks a former teacher for a gift evidently received during his convalescence. His letter is a rough draft, including one misspelling and one usage error, and lacking certain punctuation marks, and may closely resemble the rough drafts of his classmates' letters, if such existed. It is dated "Feb. 20 1951" and reads: "Dear Miss R., Thank you for the book. I am out of the hospital and I dont have to wear krutchs anymore Love Stephen."

Passing Wind

She didn't know if it was him or the dog. It wasn't her. The dog was lying there on the living room rug between them, she was on the sofa, and her visitor, rather tense, was sunk deep in a low armchair, and the smell, rather gentle, came into the air. She thought at first that it was him and she was surprised, because people don't pass wind in company very often, or at least not in a noticeable way. As they went on talking, she went on thinking it was him. She felt a little sorry for him, because she thought he was embarrassed and nervous to be with her and that was why he had passed wind. Then it occurred to her very suddenly that it might not have been him at all, it might have been the dog, and worse, if it had been the dog, he might think it had been her. It was true that the dog had stolen an entire loaf of bread that morning, and eaten it, and might now be passing wind, something he did not do otherwise. She wanted immediately to let him know, somehow, that at least it was not her. Of course there was a chance that he had not noticed, but he was smart and alert, and since she had noticed, he probably had, too, unless he was too nervous to have noticed. The problem was how to tell him.

She could say something about the dog, to excuse it. But it might not have been the dog, it might have been him. She could not be direct and simply say, "Look, if you just farted, that's all right; I just want to be clear that it wasn't me." She could say, "The dog ate a whole loaf of bread this morning, and I think he's farting." But if it was him, and not the dog, this would embarrass him. Although maybe it wouldn't. Maybe he was already embarrassed, if it was him, and this would give him a way out of his embarrassment. But by now the smell was long gone. Maybe the dog would fart again, if it was the dog. That was the only thing she could think of—the dog would fart again, if it was the dog, and then she would simply apologize for the dog, whether or not it was the dog, and that would relieve him of his embarrassment, if it was him.

Television

1.

We have all these favorite shows coming on every evening. They say it will be exciting and it always is.

They give us hints of what is to come and then it comes and it is exciting.

If dead people walked outside our windows we would be no more excited.

We want to be part of it all.

We want to be the people they talk to when they tell what is to come later in the evening and later in the week.

We listen to the ads until we are exhausted, punished with lists: they want us to buy so much, and we try, but we don't have a lot of money. Yet we can't help admiring the science of it all.

How can we ever be as sure as these people are sure? These women are women in control, as the women in my family are not.

Yet we believe in this world.

We believe these people are speaking to us.

Mother, for example, is in love with an anchorman. And my husband sits with his eyes on a certain young reporter and waits for the camera to draw back and reveal her breasts.

After the news we pick out a quiz show to watch and then a story of detective investigation.

The hours pass. Our hearts go on beating, now slow, now faster.

There is one quiz show which is particularly good. Each week the same man is there in the audience with his mouth tightly closed and tears in his eyes. His son is coming back on stage to answer more questions. The boy stands there blinking at the television camera. They will not let him go on answering questions if he wins the final sum of a hundred and twenty-eight thousand dollars. We don't care much about the boy and we don't like the mother, who smiles and shows her bad teeth, but we are moved by the father: his heavy lips, his wet eyes.

And so we turn off the telephone during this program and do not answer the knock at the door that rarely comes. We watch closely, and my husband now presses his lips together and then smiles so broadly that his eyes disappear, and as for me, I sit back like the mother with a sharp gaze, my mouth full of gold.

2.

It's not that I really think this show about Hawaiian policemen is very good, it's just that it seems more real than my own life.

Different routes through the evening: Channels 2, 2, 4, 7, 9, or channels 13, 13, 13, 2, 2, 4, etc. Sometimes it's the police dramas I want to see, other times the public television documentaries, such as one called *Swamp Critturs*.

It's partly my isolation at night, the darkness outside, the silence outside, the increasing lateness of the hour, that makes the story on television seem so interesting. But the plot, too, has something to do with it: tonight a son comes back after many years and marries his father's wife. (She is not his mother.)

We pay a good deal of attention because these shows seem to be the work of so many smart and fashionable people.

I think it is a television sound beyond the wall, but it's the honking of wild geese flying south in the first dark of the evening.

You watch a young woman named Susan Smith with pearls around her neck sing the Canadian National Anthem before a hockey game. You listen to the end of the song, then you change the channel.

Or you watch Pete Seeger's legs bounce up and down in time to his *Reuben E. Lee* song, then change the channel.

It is not what you want to be doing. It is that you are passing the time.

You are waiting until it is a certain hour and you are in a certain condition so that you can go to sleep.

There is some real satisfaction in getting this information about the next day's weather—how fast the wind might blow and from what direction, when the rain might come, when the skies might clear—

and the exact science of it is indicated by the words "40 percent" in "40 percent chance."

It all begins with the blue dot in the center of the dark screen, and this is when you can sense that these pictures will be coming to you from a long way off.

3.

Often, at the end of the day, when I am tired, my life seems to turn into a movie. I mean my real day moves into my real evening, but also moves away from me enough to be strange and a movie. It has by then become so complicated, so hard to understand, that I want to watch a different movie. I want to watch a movie made for TV, which will be simple and easy to understand, even if it involves disaster or disability or disease. It will skip over so much, it will skip over all the complications, knowing we will understand, so that major events will happen abruptly: a man may change his mind though it was firmly made up, and he may also fall in love suddenly. It will skip all the complications because there is not enough time to prepare for major events in the space of only one hour and twenty minutes, which also has to include commercial breaks, and we want major events.

One movie was about a woman professor with Alzheimer's disease; one was about an Olympic skier who lost a leg but learned to ski again. Tonight it was about a deaf man who fell in love with his speech therapist, as I knew he would because she was pretty, though not a good actress, and he was handsome, though deaf. He was deaf at the beginning of the movie and deaf again at the end, while in the middle he heard and learned to speak with a definite regional accent. In the space of one hour and twenty minutes, this man not only heard and fell deaf again but created a successful business through his own talent, was robbed of it through a company man's treachery, fell in love, kept his woman as far as the end of the movie, and lost his virginity, which seemed to be hard to lose if one was deaf and easier once one could hear.

All this was compressed into the very end of a day in my life that as the evening advanced had already moved away from me . . .

Jane and the Cane

Mother could not find her cane. She had a cane, but she could not find her special cane. Her special cane had a handle that was the head of a dog. Then she remembered: Jane had her cane. Jane had come to visit. Jane had needed a cane to get back home. That was two years ago. Mother called Jane. She told Jane she needed her cane. Jane came with a cane. When Jane came, Mother was tired. She was in bed. She did not look at the cane. Jane went back home. Mother got out of bed. She looked at the cane. She saw that it was not the same cane. It was a plain cane. She called Jane and told her: it was not the same cane. But Jane was tired. She was too tired to talk. She was going to bed. The next morning she came with the cane. Mother got out of bed. She looked at the cane. It was the right cane. It had the head of a dog on it, brown and white. Jane went home with the other cane, the plain cane. After Jane was gone, Mother complained, she complained on the phone: Why did Jane not bring back the cane? Why did Jane bring the wrong cane? Mother was tired. Oh, Mother was so tired of Jane and the cane.

Getting to Know Your Body

If your eyeballs move, this means that you're thinking, or about to start thinking.

If you don't want to be thinking at this particular moment, try to keep your eyeballs still.

Absentminded

The cat is crying at the window. It wants to come in. You think about how living with a cat and the demands of a cat make you think about simple things, like a cat's need to come indoors, and how good that is. You think about this and you are too busy thinking about this to let the cat in, so you forget to let the cat in, and it is still at the window crying. You see that you haven't let the cat in, and you think about how odd it is that while you were thinking about the cat's needs and how good it is to live with the simple needs of a cat, you were not letting the cat in but letting it go on crying at the window. Then while you're thinking about this and how odd it is, you let the cat in without knowing you're letting the cat in. Now the cat jumps up on the counter and cries for food. You see that the cat is crying for food but you don't think of feeding it because you are thinking how odd it is that you have let the cat in without knowing it. Then you see that it's crying for food while you're not feeding it, and as you see this and think it's odd that you have not heard it cry, you feed the cat without knowing that you're feeding it.

Southward Bound, Reads
Worstward Ho

Sun in eyes, faces east, waits for van bound for south meeting plane from west. Carries book, *Worstward Ho.**

In van, heading south, sits on right or west side, sun in through windows from east. Highway crosses and recrosses meandering stream passing now northeast and now northwest under. Reads *Worstward Ho*: On. Say on. Be said on. Somehow on. Till nohow on. Said nohow on.†

---

*She waits near the highway before the entrance of HoJo's for the van going south. She is going south to meet a plane coming from the west. Waiting with her is a thin, dark-haired young woman who does not stop walking back and forth restlessly near her luggage. They are both early and wait for some time. In her purse she has two books, *Worstward Ho* and *West with the Night*. If it is quiet and she reads *Worstward Ho* on the way south, when she is fresh, she can read *West with the Night* on the way back up north, when it will be later and she will be tired.

†The van arrives and she takes care to sit on the right side, so that as they travel south the sun will not come in through her window but through the windows across the aisle from her. It is early morning, and the sun shines in through the windows

Road turning and van turning east and then north of east, sun in eyes, stops reading *Worstward Ho.*[*]

Road turning and van turning east again and south, shadow on page, reads: As now by way of somehow on where in the nowhere all together?[†]

Road and van turning briefly north, sun at right shoulder, light not in eyes but flickering on page of *Worstward Ho*, reads: What when words gone? None for what then.[‡]

Van turning off highway, sun behind, sun around and in window and onto page, does not read.

Van pointing east motionless in station, in shadow of tree,

---

from the east. Later in the day, as she returns north, she thinks, it may be late enough so that the sun will come through the windows from the west.

The highway she travels crosses and recrosses a meandering stream that passes now northeast and now northwest under her. As long as she is alone, sitting in the back of the van, she does not read but looks out the window.

Soon the van pulls up in front of a shopping mall. The restless young woman with the dark hair immediately stands up and remains standing in the aisle looking at the other passengers and out the windows. Two women board the van. They smell heavily of face powder as they walk past her to sit in the back near her. Now, since she is no longer alone, she begins to read.

The van is quiet, so she reads *Worstward Ho*. The first words are: "On. Say on. Be said on. Somehow on. Till nohow on. Said nohow on." She is not very pleased by these words.

[*]But soon after, she reads a sentence she likes better: "Whither once whence no return." After that, for a while, some sentences are pleasing and some are not.

The van travels almost due south down the highway. Sometimes it leaves the highway, the sunlight circling around behind all of them, to make a stop and pick up more passengers. At each stop, the restless young woman stands up and looks around in a commanding way. The passengers who get onto the van are mostly women.

She reads on comfortably for some miles, but when the road turns, and the van turns with it, east and then north of east, the sun is in her eyes and she cannot read *Worstward Ho*.

[†]She waits, and when the road turns east again and then south, a shadow falls on the page and she can read. With difficulty, though the light is good, she reads such words as "As now by way of somehow on where in the nowhere all together?"

[‡]If the van turns briefly north, so that the sun is at her right shoulder, the light is no longer in her eyes but flickering on the page of the book, illuminating but further confusing such already confusing words as "What when words gone? None for what then."

reads: But say by way of somehow on somehow with sight to do.*

Van pointing south and moving, reads: So leastness on.

Van turning off highway, sun behind, sun around and in window and onto page, does not read.

Van pointing east then north of east motionless, in treeless station not in shadow, sun in face, does not read.†

Van turning, sun ahead, sun around and in opposite window, shadow on page, van pointing south and moving, reads: Longing the so-said mind long lost to longing. Dint of long longing lost to longing. Said is missaid. Whenever said said said missaid.‡

---

*Now the shade of a tree by a small gas station allows her to go on to read: "But say by way of somehow on somehow with sight to do." While the driver makes a phone call, one woman leaves the van to try to find a working bathroom, fails, and returns to the van.

The van resumes going south and she reads with pleasure and some understanding: "Now for to say as worst they may only they only they." And then with more pleasure: "With leastening words say least best worse. For want of worser worst. Unlessenable least best worse." And then soon there is something a little different: "So leastward on. So long as dim still. Dim undimmed. Or dimmed to dimmer still. To dimmost dim. Leastmost in dimmost dim. Utmost dim. Leastmost in utmost dim. Unworsenable worst."

The sun in another small gas station stops her from reading, heat and brightness coming in her window, what was the west window when the van was heading south but probably must be considered the east window just at this moment. While the driver makes another phone call, two women, now, leave the van to try to find a working bathroom, fail, and return to the bus.

†The van heads south again.

‡Though she is several pages farther along, some of the words are the same again: "Next fail see say how dim undimmed to worsen. How nohow save to dimmer still. But but a shade so as when after nohow somehow on to dimmer still."

Then there is something new at the bottom of the page: "Longing the so-said mind long lost to longing. The so-missaid. So far so-missaid. Dint of long longing lost to longing."

Then a combination: "Longing that all go. Dim go."

Soon after, with confusion, she reads: "Said is missaid. Whenever said said said missaid." She misunderstands and reads again: "Whenever said said said missaid." Then a third time, and when she imagines a pause in the middle of it, she understands better.

Van turning off highway, sun behind, sun around and in window and onto page, does not read.[*]

Van turning last time back onto highway, sun ahead, sun around and in opposite window, shadow on page, reads: No once. No once in pastless now.

Van turning last time off highway, sun ahead, sun around and in window, does not read.[†]

Van farthest south motionless in shadow, pointing north, reads last words: Said nohow on.[‡]

[*]At the next stop, the van driver calls out for "folks Benson and Goodwin." The Benson couple and the single Goodwin, sitting forward in the van, identify themselves as "Two Benson and one Goodwin." It takes the driver a very long time to find their papers. While he is searching, three women, now, leave the van, find a working bathroom, and return to the van.

Now each time the van stops, it stops with the sun coming in what was the west window but is now the east window, preparing to turn right and head south into the sun again. Now she has grown used to waiting with the sun on her face and on the page and watching the asphalt outside and the other passengers inside until the van turns and goes on south.

[†]Near the end of the book, she reads: "No once. No once in pastless now," and just now the van passes a cemetery near the airport and she sees many white stone angels, their wings raised.

[‡]By the time she reaches the end of her trip south, the southernmost point in the van's route, from which it will head north again, she has finished the book, which is not long. Although she has liked many of the words that came in between, its last words, "Said nohow on," say as little to her as its first, "On. Say on. Be said on."

The Walk

A translator and a critic happened to be together in the great university town of Oxford, having been invited to take part in a conference on translation. The conference occupied all of one Saturday, and that evening they had dinner alone together, though not entirely by choice. Everyone else who had participated in the conference or attended it had departed, even the organizers. Only they had chosen to stay a second night in the rooms provided for them in the college in which the conference had taken place, a down-at-heels building with stained carpets in the hallways, a smell of mildew in the guest rooms, and creaking iron bedsteads.

The restaurant was light and airy, entirely enclosed in glass like a greenhouse. The meal was good and most of the time their conversation was lively. She asked him many questions and he talked a good deal about himself. She knew something about him, since they had corresponded now and then over the years—she had asked his help on one or two points; he had admired an essay of hers; she had praised a reminiscence of his; he had courteously included an excerpt from her latest translation in an anthology. He had a certain almost obsequious charm. He liked talking about himself, and did not ask many questions of her. She noticed the imbalance but did not mind. There was some goodwill between them, though also an underlying tension because of his negative reaction to her translation.

He felt that she kept too close to the original text. He preferred the studied cadences of an earlier version and had said so in person and in print. She felt that he admired lyricism and empty rhetorical flourishes at the expense of accuracy and faithfulness to the style of the original, which was far plainer and clearer, she said, than the flowery and obfuscating earlier version. During the conference, she had given a formal presentation of her approach and he had said nothing in response, though from her lectern she could see by the expression on his face, half amused and half scornful, and by the occasional wince, as he shifted in his seat, that his feelings were strong. For his own presentation he had chosen to discuss the language of translation criticism, including his own, mischievously—or malevolently—taking as his examples the reviews of the translations of the participants in this conference. He had caused almost all of them discomfort and embarrassment, and stung their pride, for only one of them had received no bad reviews.

When they had finished their dinner, it was still light out, since the summer solstice was only a few days away. As the sky would be light for several more hours and they had been shut up in the conference room all day, suffering some tedium at various points and some tension at others, much of it caused by him, and as they were, to some extent, anyway, enjoying each other's company, they agreed that a walk would be pleasant.

The college where the conference had been held, and the restaurant, which was near it, were a good ten minutes on foot from the center of town, and their plan was to walk into town, stroll up and down the streets a bit, and then walk back out. He had not been there for many years and was curious to see it again. She had explored it on her own for the first time when she arrived the day before, but not very thoroughly or satisfactorily, since it had been crowded with tourists and too hot under the midday sun to be comfortable. She had taken the circular tour bus twice, or rather, she had made two full circuits and one half circuit, going down the main street twice, past the botanical gardens twice, to the outlying colleges twice and in again, and out to the outlying colleges one more time in order to return to where she was staying, and so she was more familiar with the town than he was. By tacit agreement she became the guide. They both felt like the colonials they were, in the mother country, she with one accent displeasing to native ears and he with another that they would not have been able to place.

They talked steadily as they walked into town, still mostly about him, his academic position, his students, his children and how he was bringing them up, and his wife, whom he missed. He and his wife had attempted a separation, but after some weeks she had returned to him. He had, during those weeks, he said, sunk into despair. When there were two of you, you decided so many little things together, such as which room to sit in with your morning coffee. When you were alone, he said, it was so miserably difficult to make those little choices.

The streets were relatively empty, though it was a Saturday night. There were not many tourists, only a few families and couples. The pavements were clear, as though they had been swept clean of the crowds. Now and then, undergraduates in formal evening dress rushed past in a cluster or singly, on the way to a university function. He and she had the curious sense that the town was full of people, but that the people were all attending events behind closed doors and out of sight. The streets were theirs for the moment. The sun hovered low in the sky, hanging above the horizon, descending so slowly that its descent was barely perceptible, and bathing the yellow stones of the old buildings in a honey-colored light. The sky above the rooftops was vast, a pale painted blue.

At the end of a long pedestrian street paved in cobblestones, they heard a full chorus of voices traveling out on the quiet evening air. The concert was taking place in a circular, rose-colored hall. They climbed the steps to a side entrance, thinking they might slip in for the remainder of the concert. He, a cosseted youngest child, was not one to obey regulations, and although she felt in this hour somewhat like a kindly aunt indulging him and his outrageous statements, she was by habit no more law-abiding than he was. Especially here, in the mother country, feeling they were less proper than the native citizens, they would be tempted to behave less properly.

But blocking the entryway were two middle-aged, heavyset women in long skirts and stout-heeled shoes chatting and laughing together, one of whom turned to them and told them civilly but firmly that they could not enter. He and she stood still for some time next to the women, enjoying the rising and falling song while they gazed down into what had been the heart of the original university, a small, centuries-old courtyard fronted by the modest façade of the first university library.

Each of the short neighboring streets, as they continued their walk, offered the surprise of another old college, often with its own gate and spiked fence and courtyard, or some tracery or corbel or bell tower to be admired. Sometimes they both wanted to go up the same street, sometimes only one of them, when the other politely went along. She found it an interesting exercise to explore a place with a person she did not know well, following not only her own impulses but also his.

Since they had both been married for many years, strolling together like this had some of the comfortable familiarity of long habit, yet it also had some of the awkwardness of a first date, since, after all, they did not really know each other very well. He was a small man, and delicate in his motions and gestures. She took care not to walk too close to him, and thought from his slight unsteadiness now and then that he was probably taking the same care to keep a certain distance from her.

When more than an hour had passed, they decided to return to their college. Now she volunteered to lead them by a different way, for the interest of it, along a street that ran parallel to the one they had come in on and would then connect to it near their destination. She did not explain all this to him, but simply assured him that the street they were about to enter would take them back to their college. He entrusted himself to her and paid little attention to where they were going, as he continued to talk.

He spoke emphatically, using strong adverbs, often expressing indignation, and admitting that some of his opinions were, as he put it, virally jaundiced: Certain things, according to him, were flagrantly obvious, or embarrassingly inaccurate, or patently ridiculous; others, of course, were magnificent, delightful, or entrancing. Condemning a certain publishing house, he remarked—although he was not old enough to have experienced the Second World War—that in its front line, incompetence and dishonesty pullulated like trench lice among infantrymen, and that the upper-level administrators should be taken out of the trenches every so often and given something restfully self-restoring to do, like sewing pages. She was content to listen, and several times thought how perfectly suitable was this conclusion—her own relative passivity, and the mild physical exertion—to the long, trying day.

Much of the street was familiar to her from passing it three times before, when the circular tour had headed out of town, but she became a little worried ten minutes into their walk back, when she was not sure which left turn to make. After all, things had flown by relatively quickly out the window of the bus. He questioned her mildly twice and she admitted her uncertainty the second time. But when they took what turned out to be the correct left turn and correctly rejoined their original road nearly opposite the restaurant where they had had dinner, and she was enjoying a feeling of satisfaction, he did not notice where they were, and simply walked on by her side, across the street from the restaurant, until she pointed it out to him. Then he was truly astonished, as though he had imagined they were far away from that corner and she had produced it out of her jacket pocket.

Now she thought he would recognize a parallel with a scene in the book she had translated, but he did not; she thought perhaps he was too occupied with reorienting himself. In the version he preferred, the passage read:

We would return by the Boulevard de la Gare, which contained the most attractive villas in the town. In each of their gardens the moonlight, copying the art of Hubert Robert, scattered its broken staircases of white marble, its fountains, its iron gates temptingly ajar. Its beams had swept away the telegraph office. All that was left of it was a column, half shattered but preserving the beauty of a ruin which endures for all time. I would by now be dragging my weary limbs and ready to drop with sleep; the balmy scent of the lime-trees seemed a reward that could be won only at the price of great fatigue and was not worth the effort. From gates far apart the watchdogs, awakened by our steps in the silence, would set up an antiphonal barking such as I still hear at times of an evening, and among which the Boulevard de la Gare (when the public gardens of Combray were constructed on its site) must have taken refuge, for wherever I may be, as soon as they begin their alternate challenge and response, I can see it again with its lime-trees, and its pavement glistening beneath the moon.

Suddenly my father would bring us to a standstill and ask my mother—"Where are we?" Exhausted by the walk but still proud of her husband, she would lovingly confess that she had not the least idea. He would shrug his shoulders and laugh. And then, as though he had produced it with his latchkey from his waistcoat pocket, he would point out to us, where it stood before our eyes, the back-gate of our own garden, which had come, hand-in-hand with the familiar corner of the Rue du Saint-Esprit, to greet us at the end of our wanderings over paths unknown.

Since he had not noticed, she intended to mention it soon, but was at the moment more interested in pointing out to him a house they were about to pass. It had once been the home of Charles Murray, the great editor of *The Oxford English Dictionary*.

When she had arrived in this town the day before, her strongest desire had been to see, not the more famous sights, but the house in which this editor had lived while doing the better part of his work, a personal account of which she had read by his granddaughter. She had taken pains to ask each person she met if he or she knew where this house might be. No one had been able to tell her, and as she ran out of time, she had given up the idea of finding it. Then, at the end of her day of touring, just as the tour bus had reached her street for the third time and stopped to let her off by the porter's lodge of the college, the guide had said something about this same editor and his house. She was already climbing down the steps and half off the bus when she heard it, and could not question the guide further. She could not believe the house was right here, in this neighborhood where she was staying, and the next day she continued to ask each person she met where the house might be.

After she had given her talk at the conference, she was approached by a short, stout man with a preoccupied, almost angry expression who concentrated his attention on her alone, ignoring everyone around them, and asked several pertinent questions and made several concise remarks about her talk. He was modest enough not to identify himself, and when she asked him who he was, he said he had just retired as librarian of this college and would be pleased, in fact, to give her a tour of the library. Since he seemed to be a highly competent person with many facts at his disposal, she thought to ask him the question she had been asking everyone else since the day before. The librarian said that of course he knew the house—it was right across the street. And he immediately led her out to the corner and pointed. There it was, its upper story and roof showing above its brick wall, as though the librarian had taken it from his jacket pocket and set it there just to please her.

The situation was not exactly the same, of course, since the librarian had not magically brought her home but had instead produced the very house she had been looking for. But now she told the story to the critic, with whom she felt a closer companionship after walking so far with him and bringing him safely back. She thought that now he would recognize the situation, and think of their walk and the passage from the book he knew so well.

In her version, the scene read:

We would return by way of the station boulevard, which was lined by the most pleasant houses in the parish. In each garden the moonlight, like Hubert Robert, scattered its broken staircases of white marble, its fountains, its half-open gates. Its light had destroyed the Telegraph Office. All that remained was a column, half shattered but preserving the beauty of an immortal ruin. I would be dragging my feet, I would be ready to drop with sleep, the fragrance of the lindens that perfumed the air seemed a reward that could be won only at the cost of the greatest fatigue and was not worth the trouble. From gates far apart, dogs awakened by our solitary steps would send forth alternating volleys of barks such as I still hear at times in the evening and among which the station boulevard (when the public garden of Combray was created on its site) must have come to take refuge, for, wherever I find myself, as soon as they begin resounding and replying, I see it again, with its lindens and its pavement lit by the moon.

Suddenly my father would stop us and ask my mother: "Where are we?" Exhausted from walking but proud of him, she would tenderly admit that she had absolutely no idea. He would shrug his shoulders and laugh. Then, as though he had taken it from his jacket pocket along with his key, he would show us the little back gate of our own garden, which stood there before us, having come, along with the corner of the rue du Saint-Esprit, to wait for us at the end of those unfamiliar streets.

But he was more interested in the great editor, and the house, and the mailbox directly in front of the house, which had been put there especially for the editor's use and from which so many of the requests for quotations had been mailed. She thought she would comment to him on the parallel at some other time, in a letter, and then perhaps he would be amused.

It was late. The sun had at last gone down, though the sky was still filled with the lingering cool light of the solstice. After he had with some difficulty opened the front door with the unfamiliar key, they said good night inside the entrance to the college and went their separate ways, he up the stairs and she down the corridor, to their musty rooms.

It was too late for her to enjoy sitting alone in the room after the long day, as she generally liked to do; she had to be up early. But then, it was not in any case the sort of room in which to enjoy silence and rest, being so meagerly appointed, with its small, frail wardrobe, whose door kept swinging open, its inconvenient lamp, its hard, flat pillows, and that persistent smell of mold. True, the bathroom, by contrast, was fitted with old marble and porcelain, and its one narrow window looked out on a handsome garden, though even it had lacked certain necessary supplies: Soon after he arrived, the day before, while she was away touring the town, he had left a panicked note on her door, though they had not yet met, inquiring about soap.

She was not disappointed by the whole experience, she decided, as her thoughts sorted themselves out. She was in bed now, with a book open in front of her, trying to read by the inadequate lamp, but each time she returned her eyes to the page, another insistent thought occurred to her and stopped her. She would have been disappointed if she had not, in the end, seen Murray's house, or if she had not seen the library, whose alarm she nearly triggered by walking across a perfectly open space at the top of an ancient staircase. She would have been disappointed in this building if the conference room had not been so gracious, with its high ceiling and dark oak beams, and she would perhaps have been disappointed in the conference itself if one of the speakers had not shown such interesting examples of the great writer's rough drafts. She was disappointed that some of the other participants had not stayed on afterward for at least a little while, that they had, in fact, seemed to be in such a hurry to leave.

But then there was the long walk, and her changing impressions of the town, which had been so crowded, hot, and oppressive at midday the day before and was this evening so serene, with its empty streets, the hollow spaces of its courtyards and back gardens, the darkness, against the sky, of its church steeples and clock towers, with its short alleys and narrow lanes, and its soft stones that, in her memory, had reflected the sky in tints of coral, growing just a few shades dimmer, as the hours passed, in the cool night.

The peace and emptiness of the town in the evening had seemed fragile and temporary; the next day it would be submerged once again in the hot crowd. And because she had made so many circuits out of the town, by bus and then on foot, it seemed to her, too, that the weight of her experience of the town was here, at this distance from it, as though the town were always to be experienced from a distance exactly the length of those two streets which, arising here, and diverging, made their way to it.

At last her thoughts came at longer intervals and she read more than she stopped to think. She then read later than she meant to, gradually forgetting the lamp, the room, and the conference, though the walk remained, as a presence, somewhere behind or beneath her reading, until she relaxed completely and slept, no longer bothered by the hard pillow.

The next morning, when she came out with her suitcase, he was there, too, in a white summer suit slightly too ample for his small frame, standing by the porter's lodge. He and she had ordered taxis for the same hour, the day before, and the two drivers were standing by the curb chatting in the early sunlight. He was, in fact, going to the same part of town, though not to the train station, but neither of them had suggested sharing a taxi. She waited while he talked on, for a few minutes, to the porter, and then they took leave of each other again before setting off in their separate taxis. As he stepped neatly into his, his last words to her, solemn and rather portentous, she thought, were ones that nobody, as it happened, had ever spoken to her before, but that she judged were likely to be correct, since he lived on the other side of the globe: "We will probably not meet again." He then made a graceful gesture of the hand which she later could not remember exactly, and whose meaning she could not quite grasp, though it seemed to combine a farewell with a concession to some sort of inevitability, and his cab moved slowly down the street, followed, soon, by her own.

Varieties of Disturbance

I have been hearing what my mother says for over forty years and I have been hearing what my husband says for only about five years, and I have often thought she was right and he was not right, but now more often I think he is right, especially on a day like today when I have just had a long conversation on the phone with my mother about my brother and my father and then a shorter conversation on the phone with my husband about the conversation I had with my mother.

My mother was worried because she hurt my brother's feelings when he told her over the phone that he wanted to take some of his vacation time to come help them since my mother had just gotten out of the hospital. She said, though she was not telling the truth, that he shouldn't come because she couldn't really have anyone in the house since she would feel she had to prepare meals, for instance, though having difficulty enough with her crutches. He argued against that, saying "That wouldn't be the *point!*" and now he doesn't answer his phone. She's afraid something has happened to him and I tell her I don't believe that. He has probably taken the vacation time he had set aside for them and gone away for a few days by himself. She forgets he is a man of nearly fifty, though I'm sorry they had to hurt his feelings like that. A short time after she hangs up I call my husband and repeat all this to him.

My mother hurt my brother's feelings while protecting certain particular feelings of my father's by claiming certain other feelings of her own, and while it was hard for me to deny my father's particular feelings, which are well-known to me, it was also hard for me not to think there was not a way to do things differently so that my brother's offer of help would not be declined and he would not be hurt.

She hurt my brother's feelings as she was protecting my father from certain feelings of disturbance anticipated by him if my brother were to come, by claiming to my brother certain feelings of disturbance of her own, slightly different. Now my brother, by not answering his phone, has caused new feelings of disturbance in my mother and father both, feelings that are the same or close to the same in them but different from the feelings of disturbance anticipated by my father and those falsely claimed by my mother to my brother. Now in her disturbance my mother has called to tell me of her and my father's feelings of disturbance over my brother, and in doing this she has caused in me feelings of disturbance also, though fainter and different from the feelings experienced now by her and my father and those anticipated by my father and falsely claimed by my mother.

When I describe this conversation to my husband, I cause in him feelings of disturbance also, stronger than mine and different in kind from those in my mother, in my father, and respectively claimed and anticipated by them. My husband is disturbed by my mother's refusing my brother's help and thus causing disturbance in him, and by her telling me of her disturbance and thus causing disturbance in me greater, he says, than I realize, but also more generally by the disturbance caused more generally not only in my brother by her but also in me by her greater than I realize, and more often than I realize, and when he points this out, it causes in me yet another disturbance dif-

ferent in kind and in degree from that caused in me by what my
mother has told me, for this disturbance is not only for myself and
my brother, and not only for my father in his anticipated and his
present disturbance, but also and most of all for my mother herself,
who has now, and has generally, caused so much disturbance, as my
husband rightly says, but is herself disturbed by only a small part
of it.

Lonely

No one is calling me. I can't check the answering machine because I have been here all this time. If I go out, someone may call while I'm out. Then I can check the answering machine when I come back in.

Mrs. D and Her Maids

Cora, who misses them all
Nellie Bingo: our darling, but she disappeared into a sanatorium
Anna the Grump
Virginia York: not a whirlwind
Birdell Moore: old-fashioned, with warm Southern sweetness
Lillian Savage: not insulted by drunks
Gertrude Hockaday: pleasant, but a perfidious hypochondriac
Ann Carberry: feeble, old, and deaf
The "Brava": came irregularly, not to be considered a Negro
High school girl: worse than nothing
Mrs. Langley: English, and exactly what we need
Our Splendid Marion
Minnie Treadway: briefly a possibility
Anna Slocum: wished it had all been a bad dream
Shirley: like a member of the family
Joan Brown: philosopher of the condition

MRS. D

Before she is Mrs. D, she lives in the city with her little daughter and her maid, Cora. The daughter is four years old. She goes to nursery school and when at home is taken care of mainly by Cora. This leaves Mrs. D free to write and also to go out in the evenings.

Mrs. D writes short stories, some good, some less good, which she places mostly in ladies' magazines. She likes to speak of "selling" a story, and she counts on earning a little money from it to supplement her salary. She will publish a story in one of the best magazines just before she is married. The story is called "Real Romance."

MARRIAGE TO MR. D

When Mrs. D's little daughter is six, Mrs. D marries again, and becomes Mrs. D. The ceremony takes place in the country at a friend's house. It is a small wedding and the reception is out on the lawn under the trees. The season is early fall, but the women are still wearing summer dresses. The little daughter's blond hair is now cut short. Cora is not at the wedding. She no longer works for Mrs. D, but they write letters to each other.

HOUSEKEEPING

Mr. and Mrs. D set up house in a college town, where Mr. D has a job teaching. Mr. D gives his stepdaughter breakfast every morning and walks her to school. Mrs. D lingers in bed before beginning her day at the typewriter.

MRS. D HAS A BABY

After a year of marriage, Mrs. D becomes pregnant. A baby boy is born in the fall, at the Lying-In Hospital. He is strong and healthy. Mr. D is very moved. He will write a short story about a father and his small son.

CORA STILL MISSES THEM ALL

Cora writes:

Ge; Was I glade to hear from you all I would had writting you but I misslayed your address   I can tell by the exsplaination that you all are fine I would love to come out and see you all expecilly the new one I know my little girl is lovely as ever all way will be   Yes I am Working, but I hafter to make up mine whether I will stay here ore go back with my one should I had said the other people did I ever write you about them   well they was very nice from England a lawyer ore laywer whitch ever you spell it   Oh, I know you will be suprise who I am working for Now you jest; I will tell you later on   I had a little accident this summer I fell and crack my knee broke a Fibula whitch I has been layed up for 2 month but I am up and working now when are you coming to the city again   when you do please try to bring the children   when every you move drop me a line let me know I dont care how nice other people are I still think about you I wish you all could come to the city to stay   Mr D could get a job Easyer than Alphonso could out there   we have a nice house out here in the Country you know how I am about the Country   well we are doing fine did you ever meet Mike   Mrs. F boy   he is nice but I know your new one is much more nicer   My greatest Love to you all

WHY MRS. D NEEDS A MAID

Mrs. D wants a family, but she also wants to write, so she needs a maid to keep the house clean, cook and serve meals, and help care for the children. The expense of keeping a maid will be compensated by the money Mrs. D will earn writing.

ONE OF THE EARLIEST MAIDS IS ONE OF THE BEST

Our darling Nellie. All I had to struggle to attain was a perfect maid, which is our most phenomenal achievement. We can't get over our luck as she moves like a dainty angel about the house doing her duties with absolute perfection.

BUT NELLIE'S HEALTH IS NOT GOOD

We are still having maid trouble because our very sweet maid is not really strong enough for the job and is constantly out sick which makes it quite a problem to know what to do. We have had her examined by the doctor and he has told her to get X-rays taken of her lungs so we will know by the end of this week whether we can even hope to have her any more at all.

NELLIE WRITES FROM THE SANATORIUM

I hope you will forgive me for not writing to you and tell you that I am sick in the hospital. I didn't want you to worry I hope you will forgive me.

I've been in the hospital 8 months And I miss home and every one.

Im in the ward with 8 girls and like it very much we get along swell.

In December Walter father had a x ray taken and the doctor said he have Tuberculosis so I had my taken and he said I have it. Oh I wish you cold see me the first two months all I did was cry.

I am coming along fine. If you see me you wont know me.

I will send you a snapshot in my next letter. I have gas on my left side.

I dont know how long I have to stay here. I hope it wont be long cause it's lonsome.

I'm dying to see the baby.

I re'cd your Card and thanks a lot I will never forget you you been so good to me.

I dont think I will work any more not for a long time any way.

Doctor said I have to be quiet when I go home.

Give my love to the baby.

I really miss you All. Love to All. Nellie Bingo.

MRS. D ANSWERS AN AD

I am writing in response to your advertisement in today's Traveler, since I shall be hiring a maid very soon. I should be glad to have you telephone me at Kirkland 0524 if the following details about the job are of interest to you.

We are a family of four. I must spend all my mornings at my work of writing. We live in a modern, convenient house.

The job is not an easy one, since there is all the housework to be done. I like to care for the baby as much as possible myself. We all regard that as a family pleasure as well as a duty, but of course he adds greatly to the washing. We enjoy eating, and we would hope that you like to cook and know how to use leftovers in appetizing and flavorsome dishes. But we do not require fancy cooking.

Anyone who works for us will have the chance to earn regular increases as long as she continues to make the house run so smoothly that my own work is in turn made more profitable.

We need someone who has the kind of temperament to fit into our house, of course. She should be cooperative, willing to accept and put into practice new ideas, especially in handling the baby, and calm, patient and firm in dealing with him. Meals should be prompt.

I should be glad to hear from you, and the sooner the better.

Yours very sincerely.

THE IMPRESSION SHE GIVES

Mrs. D gives the impression, in her letter, that she is sensible, efficient, and well organized, and that her family life is orderly.

She likes a clean house, but she herself is casual in caring for her things—after removing a sweater, she will drop it in a heap. But she has acquired for the house, often at low prices, well-made, handsome furniture and rugs, and when she and the maid have given the house some attention it looks attractive to outsiders.

She herself is only sometimes calm, patient, and firm, but it is true that the family enjoys eating.

A BAD EXPERIENCE FOLLOWS

I have finally got rid of Anna the Grump.

MRS. D PUBLISHES A STORY

The story is called "Wonderful Visit."

TIME GOES BY

The family are now living at their third address in this college town. Mrs. D composes an ad herself, with several false starts and extensive revisions before she is satisfied with the result:

Writer couple with well-trained schoolgirl daughter and year-old baby

Writer couple who must have harmonious household with wife free for morning work

Woman writer who must be free of household problems every morning requires helper able to do all housework including personal laundry and part care baby; must be cooperative, like to cook, have high standards of cleanliness, willing to accept new ideas, calm and firm in dealing with baby. We should wish to have dinner guests about once a week and at that time have good table service. Job is not easy but return will be fair treatment

Return for heavy job will be fair dealing, definite time off, wages $16 per week to start and chance to earn quarterly increases. Kirkland 0524

THE WELL-TRAINED SCHOOLGIRL

It is true that Mrs. D's daughter is well trained, though not in all respects. She is polite and sensitive to the feelings of others. She works hard in school and earns high grades. She is not very tidy in her habits, however, and does not keep her room very neat.

She is rather beautiful, according to Mrs. D, and remarkably graceful, but not phenomenally intelligent. Mrs. D describes her to friends as a tall, tense young child, and complains that she is subject to enthusiasms and anxieties that she herself finds "very wearing." She complains about her daughter's high voice. A speech therapist may help.

She remarks that sometimes, when the child is with her, she herself "cannot behave like a civilized being."

FAIR TREATMENT, CLEANLINESS, AND NEW IDEAS

It is true that Mrs. D is fair in her treatment of her maids. She also tends to develop intensely personal relationships with them. She is inquisitive as to their lives and thoughts. This can inspire affection on the part of the maid, or resentment, depending on the maid's personality. It can lead to complicated patterns of vulnerability and subsequent ill will not always comfortable for maid or employer. Mrs. D tends to be highly critical of her maids, as she is of herself and her family.

AT FIRST MRS. D IS PLEASED WITH THE RESULTS

Mrs. D confides to a friend:

The best thing about it, the really unbelievable thing, is that she can be an excellent maid and at the same time a person capable of appreciating the kind of qualities such families as yours and ours have.

A FAMILY LIKE HERS

Mrs. D sees her family, and the families of her friends, as enlightened and sympathetic to the working classes, as well as stylish, smart, witty, and cultured as regards literature, art, music, and food. In the area of music, for instance, she and her family enjoy certain pieces by the classical composers, although they also favor the more popular musicals and, over the years, will spend Sunday afternoons listening to recordings of *Oklahoma*, *Finian's Rainbow*, *South Pacific*, and *Annie Get Your Gun*.

SOON THERE ARE PROBLEMS, HOWEVER

Just when I run into the most marvelous dream of a maid that won't happen again in a century, we sublet our apartment for six weeks and this maid doesn't want to leave town. She may be influenced by her boyfriend, a twenty-four-year-old who is somehow intellectual looking despite his position as driver of a florist wagon.

MRS. D TRIES TO BE HONEST IN RECOMMENDING HER TO OTHERS

Our maid's name is Virginia. She may not turn out to be the gem for temporary work that I had hoped I was sending you.

She is not the sort who starts out like a whirlwind.

She has a sort of nervous shyness.

She is extremely slow on laundry, but it probably wouldn't matter so much in your case since you send out more things.

She can't catch up with the ironing. But if you take a firm hand it ought not to be a problem. Also, you ought to make out a schedule for her.

MRS. D REFLECTS ON HER EXPERIENCE OF VIRGINIA AFTER LETTING HER GO

Mrs. D writes a long description of Virginia:

When she came to see me for her first interview she sat sideways on the chair not looking at me. Sometimes she looked directly at me and smiled, and then she looked intelligent and sweet, but much of the time she had a hang-dog heavy dull look to her face. Her voice was slow, rough, and hesitant, though her sentences were well formulated. She talked to me about her other job. She said to me, "Maybe I'm too conscientious, I don't know. I never seem to catch up with the ironing, I don't know. The man changes his underwear every day."

When she spoke of desserts, her eyes lit up. "I know thousands of desserts I like to make," she said.

She said she had been left alone very early and hadn't had much schooling and that was why she had happened to get into domestic service.

She and I tried to work out a good schedule. She did not want to work after putting the dinner on the table at six, but she wanted to have her own dinner before leaving, otherwise she would have to eat in a restaurant. So we tried that, but there is something extraordinarily prickly about waiting on yourself, going in and out of the kitchen, when a servant is sitting there eating. And she did eat an enormous meal.

She had a pathological interest in her own diet. She was a fiend about salads and milk and fruit, all the things that cost the most.

I missed one of the baby's blankets, the best one, which I had crocheted a border for, all around. Then one day I left the iron on all afternoon on the back porch and that's when I found the baby's blanket. She had used it to cover the ironing board. What else might she do? Too soon after, the baby's playpen came apart in her hands.

Now my distrust was deepened to a certainty: she was not the person on whom to base any permanent plans. It was also obvious that she could not keep up with the ironing or anything else.

She acted dissatisfied and glum if she stayed beyond two o'clock. I had to sympathize, because what she wanted to do was go to the YWCA, where she and a few of the other domestics were taking some very improving courses.

All her friends were urging her to get a job in a defense plant. I asked her about it and she said, "The girls all say I'm wrong, but I just don't think I'd like factory work."

I was rushing around most of the morning when I should have been at the typewriter. I offered her the full-time position because the one time we had company she did such a fine job. She put on a beautiful dinner, exquisitely arranged and well cooked and perfectly served. The whole thing went off exceedingly well. But she calculated that the full-time job wouldn't be worth it to her. She also told me that if she took the full-time job she didn't see how she could get her Christmas shopping done. That was the crowning remark.

Her experience of our household was not at its easiest. We were moving at the time, and we were still not settled before I had to rush to finish a story. But she could not see that this was a chance to make herself useful to a coming writer who could thereafter afford to pay her better.

MRS. D, THE "COMING WRITER"

It is not clear what Mrs. D's ambitions are. She writes easily and fluently, and has no difficulty conceiving plots for her stories. Over lunch she and Mr. D often exchange ideas for stories or characters, though Mr. D rarely has time now to write fiction. Mrs. D's plots often involve domestic situations like her own. The characters, usually including a husband and wife, are skillfully and sympathetically drawn; they have complex relationships with recognizable small frictions, hurts, and forgiveness. She is particularly good with the speech of young children. However, the stories often have a vein of wistful sentimentality that works to their detriment.

Her approach to writing is practical. She will "capture" certain qualities in a character, a change will take place, there will be small epiphanies. When the story is done, she will try to sell it to the highest class of magazine, or the one with the best rates. The cash often makes a difference in the family's economy.

MRS. D'S CREATIVITY

Mrs. D spends her energies on many other creative projects besides writing. She sews clothes for the children, knits sweaters, bakes bread, devises unusual Christmas cards, and plans and oversees the children's craft projects. She takes pleasure in this creativity, but her pleasure itself is rather intense and driven.

96

HOPE FOR BETTER THINGS TO COME

Mrs. D writes:

Now we are looking forward to the new maid, Birdell, who will be starting Saturday. She promises to have all the warm Southern sweetness and flexibility of the old-fashioned Negro servant.

BIRDELL DOES NOT WORK OUT. ANOTHER PROSPECT IS LILLIAN

According to herself, Lillian Savage can do anything from picking up after the children to setting out a tasty snack to "swanky" stuff like typewriting and answering the phone or even taking dictation. She says: "You have to be good-natured to take a domestic job. Nothing flusters me. You'd be surprised at what I've taken from men that get to drinking, and I know how to handle it; I don't get insulted."

PERFIDY

Lillian seems like a good possibility, but then an old employer wants her back. Gertrude is going to help out and fix it so that Lillian can come anyway, but then she doesn't call and Lillian doesn't call. After the matter of Ann Carberry, neither one of them ever calls Mrs. D again.

MRS. D REFLECTS ON GERTRUDE, WHO DIDN'T WORK OUT

She was always pleasant, but was often home with various diseases—colds, etc. Once, she stayed home because, thinking she was getting a cold, she took a heavy dose of physic and it gave her cramps in the stomach and brought on her "sickness" two weeks early. The next time she had an inflammation of the eye; she thought maybe it was a stye. It was terribly inflamed. The doctor put drops on it which stung terribly but helped. The doctor said not to go to her job for fear of infection. She felt fine but supposed she'd have to do what the doctor said.

Her husband had health problems, too. She talked a lot about his bad physical condition and his stopped-up bowels.

Then he got drafted. Well, that was that for her—she wouldn't be working for me any more. He was set on making her stay with his relatives while he was gone and she was not strong enough to resist. She would just have to work for nothing in the boarding house and be part of family quarrels which she hated and which made her ill. She was a very attractive and interesting personality. Any attractive white girl who was willing to do other people's housework at a time like this was bound to be interesting for some reason.

FURTHER REFLECTIONS, INCLUDING ANNOYING THINGS ABOUT GERTRUDE

She would leave the house in terrible shape: diapers on the floor, the bathroom strewn with everything, all the baby's clothes, wet diapers, socks and shoes and unwashed rubber pants. The tub was dirty, the towels and washcloths and the baby's playthings were all over, the soap was in the water, and the water was even still standing in the tub. She left thick cold soapy water in the washing machine and tubs, diapers out of the water, and the bucket was never upstairs.

She would make pudding using good eggs, when we were out of freshly made cookies.

She was always grabbing dish towels for everything, throwing them toward the cellar door when they were too dirty, along with others that had been used maybe once. She left ashes around in all sorts of dishes, such as the salt dishes.

Then she went and recommended a maid who was too old, feeble, and deaf for the job.

MRS. D'S WORK HABITS

Mrs. D likes to start work as early in the morning as she can. Once the children are taken care of, she sits down at her typewriter and begins to type. She types fast and steadily, and the sound is loud, the table rattling and the carriage bell ringing at the end of every line. There is only an occasional silence when she pauses to read over what she has just written. She makes many changes, which involve moving the carriage back a little, x-ing out the word or phrase, rolling the carriage down a little, and inserting an emendation above the line.

She makes a carbon copy of each page, and she types both her first drafts and the copies on cheap yellow paper, aligning a piece of yellow paper, a piece of carbon paper, and another piece of yellow paper, and rolling them together into the carriage. Her fingers, with their carefully applied clear nail polish, sometimes become smudged with ink from the typewriter ribbon or with carbon from the carbon paper.

Mrs. D sits at her worktable with good upright posture. She has full, dark-brown, medium-length hair with gentle curls in it and combed to one side. She has dark eyes, round and naturally rosy cheeks, an upturned nose, and nicely shaped lips to which she applies lipstick. She wears no other makeup except, occasionally, some powder when she goes out. She looks younger than she is. She dresses nicely, usually in a skirt, blouse, and cardigan, even when alone at the typewriter.

MRS. D MAKES ANOTHER ATTEMPT

Mrs. D writes:

We are in the throes of trying to get a maid to take with us to the summer cottage.

THE SUMMER COTTAGE

Mrs. D has found a reasonably cheap cottage close to the sea where they can spend the summer. It is not a very long drive from the college town. Mrs. D goes out to the place ahead of time and puts in a good-size garden. Because of the garden, they are allowed extra gas for the move out there. Gas has been rationed because of the war.

Once they are settled, Mrs. D urges friends to come stay with them. But these friends will probably take the train: there is now a ban on pleasure driving because of the shortage of gas. They are allowed to use the car if they are going to buy food, so they may plan a food shopping trip around picking up a friend at the station. They are also allowed to use the car if they are going clamming.

Later in the summer, the ban on pleasure driving will be lifted and they will immediately drive to the ocean for a swim.

DRAFTS OF A LETTER TO AN AGENCY, WRITTEN FROM THE SEASIDE

My dear Miss McAllister,

I find it impossible to keep Ann Carberry whom you sent me through Gertrude Hockaday last week. She has tried, and in many ways she is quite satisfactory. She keeps the kitchen in fine condition and enjoys figuring out ways to use the available food to make tasty meals. But this about uses up all her time and energy; she does not step out of the kitchen on some days except to take her afternoon rest.

Which leaves, of course, the main need unsatisfied: the care of the baby.

It has been necessary for me to do all the washing, and all of his care except for giving him his meals. And she is seventy years old.

Her age, her feebleness, and her deafness combine to make her quite unsuitable for this job

nor did she ever notice a full wastebasket standing at the head of the stairs.

She is a very sweet person, very eager to please. She seems to enjoy cooking. She likes to cook her specialties, such as Parker House rolls, and I think she would suit an elderly family who could afford to pay a high wage for the light work of which she

100

and in a place where there were no other more pressing duties

would be very welcome in a house where other pressing duties need not be neglected to make these treats, such as Parker House rolls. Because of these weaknesses which made her obviously very fluttery and apprehensive, I had not the heart to break the news to her suddenly. I thank you for your kind cooperation with Gertrude in finding me any maid at all.

TWO WEEKS

Ann works for one week and is then given a week's notice.

SOME OTHER ANNOYING THINGS ABOUT ANN

She became dizzy-headed if she kept going all day.
    She snored.
    She panted when serving at the table.

ANN'S PARTING WISDOM

Ann comes in with a very small tray and remarks: "They say an ounce of help is worth a pound of pity."

THE BRAVA

Mrs. D writes:
    We now have a little Brava girl aged fourteen. She is colored, but not regarded as Negro—she must be treated as Portuguese.
    She is wonderful with the baby and can do dishes and other simple things. So far, however, she has been very irregular in her comings.

BUT AFTER THE BRAVA

Mrs. D is distressed. She has no help. She cannot write. Her family requires a great deal of work, and she is with them too much. She confides to a friend:

I am without a smitch of hired help. I cannot even behave myself like a civilized being, much less do any writing. The main reason of course is over-work on my part.

And to another:

I am in a complete state of jitters, due to the search for a maid.

And to another:

We have been intending to get in touch with your friend but haven't had company for quite a while because of our maid crisis. I should improve greatly this next year if I only get some help. I am not too sanguine about that.

FAMILY FINANCES

Mr. and Mrs. D, always short of money, have debts they must pay. One of their debts is to a friend named Bill. Bill himself is now in straitened circumstances and politely tells them that he must have the money back.

The two children are now enrolled in the same private school, one in fifth grade and the other in nursery school. Mrs. D asks the director for a tuition reduction, and he grants the children half scholarships.

MRS. D TRIES A HIGH SCHOOL GIRL

Mrs. D writes:

We got a little High School girl but she was worse than nothing.

MR. D DOES NOT HAVE TIME TO WRITE

Mr. D teaches three days a week, and on each day he teaches three classes. He has 150 themes to correct each week. His students are very bright.

THE ENGLISHWOMAN

One of Mr. D's colleagues recommends a cleaning woman. Mrs. D writes:

With his tips as to her temperament, I was able to apply the right pressure when I called up, and now she is with us. Our fingers are crossed as we say it. She is—if I can believe my luck—exactly what we need. She likes to go ahead without any instruction and she adores to work for disorderly people because, as she says, "they appreciate coming in and finding things clean and neat." She is English, experienced, quick and able. Her name is Mrs. Langley.

ALL GOES WELL, FOR A TIME

Mrs. Langley is downstairs in the playroom ironing.

BUT MRS. LANGLEY WILL NOT STAY

Mrs. Langley has left us.

MISCARRIAGE

Mrs. D has been trying to have another baby, but she miscarries early in the pregnancy. It is her third miscarriage. But she will not give up.

OUR SPLENDID MARION

For a time they are joined by what Mrs. D considers a wonderful girl, a nineteen-year-old commercial-college student. She lifts an enormous load from their shoulders, but they worry because she seems to have a life of all work and no play and never sees boys.

Then she, too, goes on her way.

MRS. D SEES A DOCTOR

Mrs. D consults a doctor about her trouble conceiving. She tells him that an earlier doctor had helped her to conceive by blowing some sort of gas into her.

MR. AND MRS. D ARE BOTH WRITING

Mrs. D will be having a story published soon, and she has just finished writing another one, after working every day from 9:30 to 3:00. As for Mr. D, he is not writing stories anymore, but he has begun writing articles.

They hope her latest story will sell, too, because they find themselves without much money.

MRS. D IS PREGNANT AGAIN

Again Mrs. D places an ad, shorter this time:

> COOK-HOUSEKEEPER—12 noon to early dinner, in considerate home. No washing, no Sunday work. $20 week. Tel. 2997.

MINNIE ANSWERS IN FLOWERY HANDWRITING

Regarding the enclosed "ad" does it mean I may have a room in your house, or does it refer to one who has a home, and who would come in each week day to fill your needs? I did not just understand from the wording of the "ad" just the conditions so thought I'd inquire and if interested I'd like to hear from you if the position has not been taken and details of duties.

MINNIE WILL BE GIVEN A CHANCE. SHE WRITES TO ACCEPT

Your gracious letter at hand and I hope my earnest efforts may prove satisfactory, and of course I expect to consult with you as to your wishes regarding all things pertaining to your home management. My idea, after I become familiar with things, is to relieve you as much as I can, so you may have more freedom to care for your health, and other duties of your own. I very much appreciate the fact that you have not asked for references etc. as I prefer to come on my own merits, yet it is a gracious gesture on your part to receive into your home an entire stranger, with no introduction except our correspondence.

I hope I may prove worthy of your confidence and that I may soon adjust myself to your house hold.

MINNIE DOES NOT WORK OUT, AND SOON THEREAFTER MRS. D DECIDES TO HIRE A GIRL FROM A RESIDENTIAL SCHOOL FOR DELINQUENT CHILDREN

Mrs. D receives a letter from the Field Worker, Miss Anderson:

There are many matters to be considered before we could place a girl permanently in your home, and at the present time I do not have a suitable girl available.

MRS. D PERSISTS IN ASKING FOR ONE IN PARTICULAR. MISS ANDERSON ANSWERS

Anna would be glad to stay with you permanently. But I am afraid you would find that adequate supervision would be a bigger problem than you realize. I could tell you more about Anna's very poor background, and her mentality, which we have studied over a period of years, and you would then realize why our rules have to be rather severe.

For instance, there is the question of the hour she is to get in when she goes to the movies one night a week. I set this at 10:30 rather than 11:30, thinking that she should be able to go to the first show, in which case 10:30 seems late enough. She has also asked if she may attend the New Year's Dance at the White Eagle Dance Hall with her girl friend and their escorts. Knowing nothing of the type of dance this will be, I hesitate to grant this privilege. These requests are just a sample of the problems which would increase as time went on. We want our girls to be contented and lead as normal a life as possible, but they must be protected.

MRS. D PERSISTS. MISS ANDERSON YIELDS

As soon as I hear that a definite transfer has been accomplished I will send you a contract, and will contact the Welfare Department.

After discussing matters in detail we can probably be a bit more lenient, but success depends a great deal on her outside contacts, and she will need a great deal of guidance, as is the case with many of our state's unfortunate girls.

DESPITE HIGH HOPES ON THE PART OF ALL CONCERNED, ANNA'S EMPLOYMENT IS NOT A SUCCESS

Mrs. D writes:

It is so hard to keep Anna in bounds, for even under this watching she managed to connive with a taxi driver and take our youngest out to visit friends of hers at a long distance and feed him Lord knows what.

She may also have been making indiscreet gestures downtown.

BACK AT THE SCHOOL

Anna writes:

Sorry not to have answered long before now, but we can write only one letter a week which is on Sundays.

How is everyone down that way. It sure is quite a lost to me.

The snow storm we had a week ago, didn't have too much effect on our trip here. There was 2–4 inches of snow in Some places. Miss Anderson wished she had some chains that day. Cars slid from one side of the road to the other, and one car went off on the wrong side of the road into a ditch. Several had to get out of the car to clean off windshiels and I don't know what. We stopped at the Rutland Dairy Bar for lunch, and then from there we had good weather.

Hope your trip was as successful as that of ours.

The points of view which you had mentioned in your letter are all very true and I only wished it had been a bad dream myself.

Glad to know you called Evelyn and Mrs. Warner. I can imagine how they felt and by all means Evelyn. She and I thought quite a lot of each other and I sure miss her. I miss church chior and M. Y. F. very much.

Close now with best wishes.

MRS. D FINDS ANOTHER GIRL SHE LIKES FROM THE SCHOOL
AND RECEIVES A CONTRACT FOR HER HIRE AND SUPERVISION

Unless wages for your present girl are paid in full to date of return or transfer no other girl will be placed with you until full settlement of all accounts is made.

You will not hire this girl out to any other party.

You are to exercise parental supervision with due consideration for physical health and cleanliness, moral training, improvement of mind and wise use of leisure time.

If girl does not prove satisfactory you will notify the school at once and she will be returned. The school also reserves the right to return the she any time the school sees fit.

You will promptly advise the Priest or Minister of the Church with which she is affiliated, as to her arrival in your community.

You will supervise the buying of her clothing and all other necessary articles and you will allow her a small amount of spending money, not more than $1.00 cents per week. Her wages will be $15 per week.

MRS. D GIVES BIRTH TO A HEALTHY, FULL-TERM BABY.
SHE SENDS THE SCHOOL A GOOD REPORT OF SHIRLEY

Shirley has been wonderful all through my hospitalization and since my return home. Thanks to her I have had a good rest and shall be able to pick up my various responsibilities eagerly as soon as we get a little cool weather.

We have managed to get Shirley into a swimming hole for most of the hot afternoons.

MRS. D SUPERVISES AS SHIRLEY BUYS CLOTHES

On the July 31 bill: raincoat, hairbrush, suit, skirt, jacket, underpants, gym suit.

On the August 31 bill: sweater, dickey, wool skirt, blouses, sneakers, blue jeans.

MEANWHILE, ANNA WRITES FROM HER NEW POSITION IN CONNECTICUT

I said I would write and let you know where I went, when I got a new job, so here I am. I am working in Conn. They are lovely people and they take me with them most every place they go. I have a very nice room with a little radio, electric fan, private bath room with hot and cold water, and etc.

We are near the salt water beach, and go swimming 2 or 3 times a week, and we sure injoy it, as it's so hot every day here, that we can hardly breath, and the humidity very heavy with out any stirring in the air that we all lie around like sticks.

Last Sunday, there was 8,500 people and children at the beach. What do you think of that.

I walk nearly 4 to 6 miles when I go shopping or movies, etc., both ways altogether. Except when they go in by the car.

I am partly on my own here, and next month I will be having all my own money. I don't have to send any of my mail back to the school. The last letter I got from home was about a month ago saying that they were having nothing more to do with me because I wouldn't stop writting letters to my brother in the service. I just couldn't stop that for anyone as I think too much of that brother. I have written home to them twice with in the last 3 weeks and no answer. They won't even let my sisters write to me any more.

Well I am so glad to think that I am out again and hope to hold it out.

I am so glad to know that you are adoring your little baby girl. I can see your reason if you take to them the way I do.

Write soon.

AFTER A YEAR, SHIRLEY IS STILL WITH MRS. D

It is an entirely satisfactory situation.

BUT MRS. D WORRIES ABOUT SHIRLEY'S SENSITIVITY AND HER FAMILY BACK HOME

Life isn't easy for a girl like Shirley, sensitive and loving and having to give up a family whom it is natural for her to care about.

THE FIELD WORKER IS NOT SURE SHIRLEY SHOULD TAKE ON AN ADDITIONAL JOB

Shirley requests permission to work Sunday afternoons in a luncheonette as waitress. Without knowing more particulars concerning the reputation of the luncheonette, the clientele, etc., I hesitate to give her permission. However if all is in order in that respect, and if such work would not interfere with her duties in your home and with her school work, I have no objection to her earning a little extra money in this way. However she must remember that her first obligation is to you.

TROUBLE: SHIRLEY EXPLAINS TO MRS. D

Mrs. D; I lied to you about the Sunday night altogether. I was with Dixie, Dolores, & a soldier named Jimmie who I met before we left for the Cape. I didn't think it would sound so suspicious to be out to dinner with Dixie, but I guess it sounded worse. You would probably think it was a pick-up, so I'm not going to try to argue out of it. As far as doing anything else underhanded, I've only been out once a week, so I don't see how I could possibly do anything so terrible. I have missed Church about 3 times, maybe 4. Only two of the times I have helped out at the Maples. The other times I have waited for Tootsie & Ralph to come after me when they got out of Church. One of the days that I said I had to stay after school I didn't. I went riding with Judy.

Mr. Russell talked to me about it. He said to be "above board" with you, so I'm telling you everything. I can't think of anything else I have done underhanded. Since last Thurs. I've tried to be very nice & happy with everyone but I'm not at all. If I can't even go home to see my mother & family things must be in pretty bad shape. I haven't been home since the last of Dec. I would like to see everybody.

I have learned a lesson Mrs. D and I'll never lie to you again. I would be the happiest person, if you would give me another chance to work at the Maples. I want to very much because you wouldn't have to give me any money then. I hate to ask you for it, and I do need it. I don't like you to have to pay my cleaning bills, & money for the bus & things like that, that I have to ask you for all the time. You wouldn't even have to give me an allowance. I promise you with my whole heart that you wouldn't regret it. If you say be home at six-thirty I'd be home if I had to leave everything in a mess. Ray told me when he called today that the girls who work there said they never missed anyone as they missed me sunday. I couldn't get a job any-where and make as good money as I do there, one day a week. I only want to work on Sundays, & no other place would want a person who could work just that time. Beckmann's only pay 45 ¢ an hr. & the Walkers pay 60 ¢ besides the tips. Lots of the kids from high school came down that sunday, because I was working & it certainly helps the business. It is hard work but I love it, and would never complain about being tired. Ray also told me that Dixie wasn't putting anyone on steady for Sundays, because he was waiting to see if I could come back. Dixie knows why I can't do it anyway, because I told him why I'm here. He would be willing to help me, I know. I'm begging you for this one chance, and if it doesn't work, I'll go back to the school. I'd hate to but I would be willing to go if I knew I did something wrong.

Shirley

SHIRLEY IS FORGIVEN, BUT EVENTUALLY LEAVES MRS. D OF HER OWN ACCORD. AFTER SHIRLEY, THERE IS JOAN BROWN, THOUGH NOT FOR LONG

From her new job, Joan sends a note to Mrs. D's little boy:

Everyone has their ups and downs. At our house, they are nearly all downs. I guess its the same at yours.

I really enjoyed working at your house, and I didn't really understand myself, for more or less wanting to leave. But it is much more pleasant working at a store.

You shall never know how I feel about doing housework all the time, as you shall probably never experience it.

HOW MANY MAIDS WILL MRS. D HAVE IN HER LIFETIME?

Mrs. D will have at least one hundred maids in her lifetime. At a certain point she stops calling them maids and begins to call them cleaning women. They don't live in her house, but come in from outside.

AFTER JOAN IS LONG GONE, MRS. D WRITES TO A FRIEND

What I am doing is trying to start a new cleaning woman digging out some of the accumulations of this and that.

NAMES OF SOME LATER MAIDS, WITH CHARACTERISTICS

Ingrid from Austria, with them for a year: moved to Switzerland
Doris: came to clean twice a week
Mrs. Tuit, pronounced "Toot": was hit on the head by a music stand
Anne Foster: lost a ring at the beach
Mrs. Bushey: deaf as a doorpost

20 Sculptures in One Hour

1.

The problem is to see 20 sculptures in one hour. An hour seems like a long time. But 20 sculptures are a lot of sculptures. Yet an hour still seems like a long time. When we calculate, we discover that one hour divided by 20 sculptures gives us three minutes a sculpture. But though the calculation is correct, this seems wrong to us: three minutes is far too little time in which to see a sculpture, and it is also far too little to be left with, after starting with a whole hour. The trouble, we suppose, is that there are so many sculptures. Yet however many sculptures there are, we still feel we ought to have enough time if we have an hour. It must be that although the calculation is correct, it does not represent the situation correctly, though how to represent the situation correctly in terms of a calculation, and why this calculation does not really represent it, we can't yet discover.

2.

The answer may be this: one hour is really much shorter than we have become accustomed to believe, and three minutes much longer, so that we may eventually reverse our problem and say that we start with a fairly short period of time, one hour, in which to see 20 sculptures, and find after calculation that we will have a surprisingly long period of time, three minutes, in which to look at each sculpture, although at this point it may begin to seem wrong that so many periods lasting so long, three minutes each, can all be contained in so short a period, one hour.

Nietszche

Oh, poor Dad. I'm sorry I made fun of you.
Now I'm spelling Nietszche wrong, too.

What You Learn About
the Baby

IDLE

You learn how to be idle, how to do nothing. That is the new thing in your life—to do nothing. To do nothing and not be impatient about doing nothing. It is easy to do nothing and become impatient. It is not easy to do nothing and not mind it, not mind the hours passing, the hours of the morning passing and then the hours of the afternoon, and one day passing and the next passing, while you do nothing.

WHAT YOU CAN COUNT ON

You learn never to count on anything being the same from day to day, that he will fall asleep at a certain hour, or sleep for a certain length of time. Some days he sleeps for several hours at a stretch, other days he sleeps no more than half an hour.

Sometimes he will wake suddenly, crying hard, when you were prepared to go on working for another hour. Now you prepare to stop. But as it takes you a few minutes to end your work for the day, and you cannot go to him immediately, he stops crying and continues quiet. Now, though you have prepared to end work for the day, you prepare to resume working.

DON'T EXPECT TO FINISH ANYTHING

You learn never to expect to finish anything. For example, the baby is staring at a red ball. You are cleaning some large radishes. The baby will begin to fuss when you have cleaned four and there are eight left to clean.

YOU WILL NOT KNOW WHAT IS WRONG

The baby is on his back in his cradle crying. His legs are slightly lifted from the surface of his mattress in the effort of his crying. His head is so heavy and his legs so light and his muscles so hard that his legs fly up easily from the mattress when he tenses, as now.

Often, you will wonder what is wrong, why he is crying, and it would help, it would save you much disturbance, to know what is wrong, whether he is hungry, or tired, or bored, or cold, or hot, or uncomfortable in his clothes, or in pain in his stomach or bowels. But you will not know, or not when it would help to know, at the time, but only later, when you have guessed correctly or many times incorrectly. And it will not help to know afterward, or it will not help unless you have learned from the experience to identify a particular cry that means hunger, or pain, etc. But the memory of a cry is a difficult one to fix in your mind.

WHAT EXHAUSTS YOU

You must think and feel for him as well as for yourself—that he is tired, or bored, or uncomfortable.

SITTING STILL

You learn to sit still. You learn to stare as he stares, to stare up at the rafters as long as he stares up at the rafters, sitting still in a large space.

ENTERTAINMENT

For him, though not usually for you, merely to look at a thing is an entertainment.

Then, there are some things that not just you, and not just he, but both of you like to do, such as lie in the hammock, or take a walk, or take a bath.

RENUNCIATION

You give up, or postpone, for his sake, many of the pleasures you once enjoyed, such as eating meals when you are hungry, eating as much as you want, watching a movie all the way through from beginning to end, reading as much of a book as you want to at one sitting, going to sleep when you are tired, sleeping until you have had enough sleep.

You look forward to a party as you never used to look forward to a party, now that you are at home alone with him so much. But at this party you will not be able to talk to anyone for more than a few minutes, because he cries so constantly, and in the end he will be your only company, in a back bedroom.

QUESTIONS

How do his eyes know to seek out your eyes? How does his mouth know it is a mouth, when it imitates yours?

HIS PERCEPTIONS

You learn from reading it in a book that he recognizes you not by the appearance of your face but by your smell and the way you hold him, that he focuses clearly on an object only when it is held a certain distance from him, and that he can see only in shades of gray. Even what is white or black to you is only a shade of gray to him.

THE DIFFICULTY OF A SHADOW

He reaches to grasp the shadow of his spoon, but the shadow reappears on the back of his hand.

HIS SOUNDS

You discover that he makes many sounds in his throat to accompany what is happening to him: sounds in the form of grunts, air expelled in small gusts. Then sometimes high squeaks, and then sometimes, when he has learned to smile at you, high coos.

PRIORITY

It should be very simple: while he is awake, you care for him. As soon as he goes to sleep, you do the most important thing you have to do, and do it as long as you can, either until it is done or until he wakes up. If he wakes up before it is done, you care for him until he sleeps again, and then you continue to work on the most important thing. In this way, you should learn to recognize which thing is the most important and to work on it as soon as you have the opportunity.

ODD THINGS YOU NOTICE ABOUT HIM

The dark gray lint that collects in the lines of his palm.

The white fuzz that collects in his armpit.

The black under the tips of his fingernails. You have let his nails get too long, because it is hard to make a precise cut on such a small thing constantly moving. Now it would take a very small nailbrush to clean them.

The colors of his face: his pink forehead, his bluish eyelids, his reddish-gold eyebrows. And the tiny beads of sweat standing out from the tiny pores of his skin.

When he yawns, how the wings of his nostrils turn yellow.

When he holds his breath and pushes down on his diaphragm, how quickly his face turns red.

His uneven breath: how his breath changes in response to his motion, and to his curiosity.

How his bent arms and legs, when he is asleep on his stomach, take the shape of an hourglass.

When he lies against your chest, how he lifts his head to look around like a turtle and drops it again because it is so heavy.

How his hands move slowly through the air like crabs or other sea creatures before closing on a toy.

How, bottom up, folded, he looks as though he were going away, or as though he were upside down.

CONNECTED BY A SINGLE NIPPLE

You are lying on the bed nursing him, but you are not holding on to him with your arms or hands and he is not holding on to you. He is connected to you by a single nipple.

DISORDER

You learn that there is less order in your life now. Or if there is to be order, you must work hard at maintaining it. For instance, it is evening and you are lying on the bed with the baby half asleep beside you. You are watching *Gaslight*. Suddenly a thunderstorm breaks and the rain comes down hard. You remember the baby's clothes out on the line, and you get up from the bed and run outdoors. The baby begins crying at being left so abruptly half asleep on the bed. *Gaslight* continues, the baby screams now, and you are out in the hard rainfall in your white bathrobe.

PROTOCOL

There are so many occasions for greetings in the course of his day. Upon each waking, a greeting. Each time you enter the room, a greeting. And in each greeting there is real enthusiasm.

DISTRACTION

You decide you must attend some public event, say a concert, despite the difficulty of arranging such a thing. You make elaborate preparations to leave the baby with a babysitter, taking a bag full of equipment, a folding bed, a folding stroller, and so on. Now, as the concert proceeds, you sit thinking not about the concert but only about the elaborate preparations and whether they have been adequate, and no matter how often you try to listen to the concert, you will hear only a few minutes of it before thinking again about those elaborate preparations and whether they have been adequate to the comfort of the baby and the convenience of the babysitter.

HENRI BERGSON

He demonstrates to you what you learned long ago from reading Henri Bergson—that laughter is always preceded by surprise.

YOU DO NOT KNOW WHEN HE WILL FALL ASLEEP

If his eyes are wide open staring at a light, it does not mean that he will not be asleep within minutes.

If he cries with a squeaky cry and squirms with wiry strength against your chest, digging his sharp little fingernails into your shoulder, or raking your neck, or pushing his face into your shirt, it does not mean he will not relax in five minutes and grow heavy. But five minutes is a very long time when you are caring for a baby.

WHAT RESEMBLES HIS CRY

Listening for his cry, you mistake, for his cry, the wind, seagulls, and police sirens.

TIME

It is not that five minutes is always a very long time when you are caring for a baby but that time passes very slowly when you are waiting for a baby to go to sleep, when you are listening to him cry alone in his bed or whimper close to your ear.

Then time passes very quickly once the baby is asleep. The things you have to do have always taken this long to do, but before the baby was born it did not matter, because there were many such hours in the day to do these things. Now there is only one hour, and again later, on some days, one hour, and again, very late in the day, on some days, one last hour.

ORDER

You cannot think clearly or remain calm in such disorder. And so you learn to wash a dish as soon as you use it, otherwise it may not be washed for a very long time. You learn to make your bed immediately because there may be no time to do it later. And then you begin to worry regularly, if not constantly, about how to save time. You learn to prepare for the baby's waking as soon as the baby sleeps. You learn to prepare everything hours in advance. Then your conception of time begins to change. The future collapses into the present.

OTHER DAYS

There are other days, despite what you have learned about saving time, and preparing ahead, when something in you relaxes, or you are simply tired. You do not mind if the house is untidy. You do not mind if you do nothing but care for the baby. You do not mind if time goes by while you lie in the hammock and read a magazine.

WHY HE SMILES

He looks at a window with serious interest. He looks at a painting and smiles. It is hard to know what that smile means. Is he pleased by the painting? Is the painting funny to him? No, soon you understand that he smiles at the painting for the same reason he smiles at you: because the painting is looking at him.

A PROBLEM OF BALANCE

A problem of balance: if he yawns, he falls over backward.

MOVING FORWARD

You worry about moving forward, or about the difference between moving forward and staying in one place. You begin to notice which things have to be done over and over again in one day, and which things have to be done once every day, and which things have to be done every few days, and so on, and all these things only cause you to mark time, stay in one place, rather than move forward, or, rather, keep you from slipping backward, whereas certain other things are done only once. A job to earn money is done only once, a letter is written saying a thing only once and never again, an event is planned that will happen only once, news is received or news passed along only once, and if, in this way, something happens that will happen only once, this day is different from other days, and on this day your life seems to move forward, and it is easier to sit still holding the baby and staring at the wall knowing that on this day, at least, your life has moved forward; there has been a change, however small.

A SMALL THING WITH ANOTHER THING, EVEN SMALLER

Asleep in his carriage, he is woken by a fly.

PATIENCE

You try to understand why on some days you have no patience and on others your patience is limitless and you will stand over him for a long time where he lies on his back waving his arms, kicking his legs, or looking up at the painting on the wall. Why on some days it is limitless and on others, or at other times, late in a day when you have been patient, you cannot bear his crying and want to threaten to put him away in his bed to cry alone if he does not stop crying in your arms, and sometimes you do put him away in his bed to cry alone.

IMPATIENCE

You learn about patience. You discover patience. Or you discover how patience extends up to a certain point and then it ends and impatience begins. Or rather, impatience was there all along, underneath a light, surface kind of patience, and at a certain point the light kind of patience wears away and all that's left is the impatience. Then the impatience grows.

PARADOX

You begin to understand paradox: lying on the bed next to him, you are deeply interested, watching his face and holding his hands, and yet at the same time you are deeply bored, wishing you were somewhere else doing something else.

REGRESSION

Although he is at such an early stage in his development, he regresses, when he is hungry or tired, to an earlier stage, still, of noncommunication, self-absorption, and spastic motion.

BETWEEN HUMAN AND ANIMAL

How he is somewhere between human and animal. While he can't see well, while he looks blindly toward the brightest light, and can't see you, or can't see your features but more clearly the edge of your face, the edge of your head; and while his movements are more chaotic; and while he is more subject to the needs of his body, and can't be distracted, by intellectual curiosity, from his hunger or loneliness or exhaustion, then he seems to you more animal than human.

HOW PARTS OF HIM ARE NOT CONNECTED

He does not know what his hand is doing: it curls around the iron rod of your chair and holds it fast. Then, while he is looking elsewhere, it curls around the narrow black foot of a strange frog.

ADMIRATION

He is filled with such courage, goodwill, curiosity, and self-reliance that you admire him for it. But then you realize he was born with these qualities: now what do you do with your admiration?

RESPONSIBILITY

How responsible he is, to the limits of his capacity, for his own body, for his own safety. He holds his breath when a cloth covers his face. He widens his eyes in the dark. When he loses his balance, his hands curl around whatever comes under them, and he clutches the stuff of your shirt.

WITHIN HIS LIMITS

How he is curious, to the limits of his understanding; how he attempts to approach what arouses his curiosity, to the limits of his motion; how confident he is, to the limits of his knowledge; how masterful he is, to the limits of his competence; how he derives satisfaction from another face before him, to the limits of his attention; how he asserts his needs, to the limits of his force.

Her Mother's Mother

1.

There are times when she is gentle, but there are also times when she is not gentle, when she is fierce and unrelenting toward him or them all, and she knows it is the strange spirit of her mother in her then. For there were times when her mother was gentle, but there were also times when she was fierce and unrelenting toward her or them all, and she knows it was the spirit of her mother's mother in her mother then. For her mother's mother had been gentle sometimes, her mother said, and teased her or them all, but she had also been fierce and unrelenting, and accused her of lying, and perhaps them all.

2.

In the night, late at night, her mother's mother used to weep and implore her husband, as her mother, still a girl, lay in bed listening. Her mother, when she was grown, did not weep and implore her husband in the night, or not where her daughter could hear her, as she lay in bed listening. Her mother later could not know, since she could not hear, whether her daughter, when she was grown, wept and implored her husband in the night, late at night, like her mother's mother.

How It Is Done

There is a description in a child's science book of the act of love that makes it all quite clear and helps when one begins to forget. It starts with affection between a man and a woman. The blood goes to their genitals as they kiss and caress each other, this swelling creates a desire in these parts to be touched further, the man's penis becomes larger and quite stiff and the woman's vagina moist and slippery. The penis can now be pushed into the woman's vagina and the parts move "comfortably and pleasantly" together until the man and woman reach orgasm, "not necessarily at the same time." The article ends, however, with a cautionary emendation of the opening statement about affection: nowadays many people make love, it says, who do not love each other, or even have any affection for each other, and whether or not this is a good thing we do not yet know.

Insomnia

My body aches so—
It must be this heavy bed pressing up against me.

Burning Family Members

First they burned her—that was last month. Actually just two weeks ago. Now they're starving him. When he's dead, they'll burn him, too.

Oh, how jolly. All this burning of family members in the summertime.

It isn't the same "they," of course. "They" burned her thousands of miles away from here. The "they" that are starving him here are different.

Wait. They were supposed to starve him, but now they're feeding him.

They're feeding him, against doctor's orders?

Yes. We had said, All right, let him die. The doctors advised it.

He was sick?

He wasn't really sick.

He wasn't sick, but they wanted to let him die?

He had just been sick, he had had pneumonia, and he was better.

So he was better and that was when they decided to let him die?

Well, he was old, and they didn't want to treat him for pneumonia again.

They thought it was better for him to die than get sick again?

Yes. Then, at the rest home, they made a mistake and gave him his breakfast. They must not have had the doctor's orders. They told us, "He's had a good breakfast!" Just when we were prepared for him to start dying.

All right. Now they've got it right. They're not feeding him anymore.

Things are back on schedule.

He'll have to die sooner or later.

He's taking a few days to do it.

It wasn't certain he would die before, when they gave him breakfast. He ate it. They said he enjoyed it! But he's beyond eating now. He doesn't even wake up.

So he's asleep?

Well, not exactly. His eyes are open, a little. But he doesn't see anything—his eyes don't move. And he won't answer if you speak to him.

But you don't know how long it will take.

A few days after that, they'll burn him.

After what?

After he dies.

You'll let them burn him.

We'll ask them to burn him. In fact, we'll pay them to burn him.

Why not burn him right away?

Before he dies?

No, no. Why did you say "a few days after that"?

According to the law, we have to wait at least forty-eight hours.

Even in the case of an innocent old accountant?

He wasn't so innocent. Think of the testimony he gave.

You mean, if he dies on a Thursday, he won't be burned until Monday.

They take him away, once he's dead. They keep him somewhere, and then they take him to where he'll be burned.

Who goes with him and keeps him company once he's dead?

No one, actually.

No one goes with him?

Well, someone will take him away, but we don't know the person.

You don't know the person?

It will be an employee.

Probably in the middle of the night?

Yes.

And you probably don't know where they'll take him either?

No.

And then no one will keep him company?

Well, he won't be alive anymore.

So you don't think it matters.

They will put him in a coffin?

No, it's actually a cardboard box.

A cardboard box?

Yes, a small one. Narrow and small. It didn't weigh much, even with him in it.

Was he a small man?

No. But as he got older he got smaller. And lighter. But still, it should have been bigger than that.

Are you sure he was in the box?

Yes.

Did you look?

No.

Why not?

They don't really give you an opportunity.

So they burned something in a cardboard box that you *trust* was your father?

Yes.

How long did it take?

Hours and hours.

Burn the accountant! What a festival!

We didn't know it would be cardboard. We didn't know it would be so small or so light.

You were "surprised."

I don't know where he has gone now that he's dead. I wonder where he is.

You're asking that now? Why didn't you ask that before?

Well, I did. I didn't have an answer. It's more urgent now.

"Urgent."

I wanted to think he was still nearby, I really wanted to believe that. If he was nearby, I thought he would be hovering.

Hovering?

I don't see him walking. I see him floating a few feet off the ground.

You say "I see him"—you can sit in a comfortable chair and say that you "see him." Where do you think he is?

But if he's nearby, hovering, is he the way he used to be, or is he the way he was at the end? He used to have all his memory. Does he get it back before he returns? Or is he the way he was near the end, with a lot of his memory gone?

What are you talking about?

At first I used to ask him a question and he would say, "No, I don't remember." Then he would just shake his head if I asked. But he had a little smile on his face, as though he didn't mind not remembering. He looked as if he thought it was interesting. He seemed to be enjoying the attention. At that time he still liked to watch things. One rainy day we sat together outside the front entrance of the home, under a sort of roof.

Wait a minute. What are you calling "the home"?

The old people's home, where he lived at the end.

That is not a home.

He watched the sparrows hopping around on the wet asphalt. Then a boy rode by on a bicycle. Then a woman walked by with a brightly colored umbrella. He pointed to these things. The sparrows, the boy on the bicycle, the woman with the colorful umbrella in the rain.

No, of course. You want to think he's still hovering nearby.

No, I don't think he's there anymore.

You may as well add that he still has his memory. He would have to. If he didn't, he would lose interest and just drift away.

I do think he was there for three days afterward, anyway. I do think that.

Why three?

The Way to Perfection

Practicing at the piano:
My Alberti basses were not even.
But did my movement float this morning?
Yes!

The Fellowship

1.

It is not that you are not qualified to receive the fellowship, it is that each year your application is not good enough. When at last your application is perfect, then you will receive the fellowship.

2.

It is not that you are not qualified to receive the fellowship, it is that your patience must be tested first. Each year, you are patient, but not patient enough. When you have truly learned what it is to be patient, so much so that you forget all about the fellowship, then you will receive the fellowship.

Helen and Vi: A Study in
Health and Vitality

Introduction

The following study presents the lives of two elderly women still thriving in their eighties and nineties. Although the account will necessarily be incomplete, depending as it does in part on the subjects' memories, it will be offered in detail whenever possible. Our hope is that, through this close description, some notion may be formed as to which aspects of the subjects' behaviors and life histories have produced such all-around physical, mental, emotional, and spiritual health.

Both women were born in America, one of African-American parents and one of immigrants from Sweden. The first, Vi, is eighty-five years old, currently still in very good health, working four days a week as a house- and office-cleaner, and active in her church. The other, Helen, ninety-two, is in good health apart from her weakened sight and hearing, and though she now resides in a nursing home, she lived alone and independently until one year ago, caring for herself and her large house and yard with minimal help. She still looks after her own hygiene and tidies her room.

Background

Both Vi and Helen grew up in intact families with other children and two caregivers (in Vi's case these were her grandparents, for many years). Both were close to their siblings (in Vi's case there were also cousins in the immediate family) and remained in close touch with them throughout their lives. Both have outlived all of them: Helen was predeceased by an older brother who reached the age of ninety and an older sister who died at seventy-eight; Vi by seven brothers, sisters and cousins, all but one of whom lived into their eighties and nineties. Her last remaining cousin died at the age of ninety-four, still going out to work as a cook.

Vi spent most of her childhood in Virginia on her grandparents' farm. She was one of eight siblings and cousins, all of whom lived with the grandparents and were raised by them up to a certain age. Her grandfather's farm was surrounded by fields and woods. The children went barefoot most of the time, so their physical contact with the land was constant, and intimate.

The children never saw a doctor. If one of them was sick, Vi's grandmother would go out into the fields or woods and find a particular kind of bark or leaf, and "boil it up." Her grandfather taught the children to recognize certain healthful wild plants, and in particular to tell the male from the female of certain flowers, since each had different properties; then they would be sent to gather the plants themselves. As a regular preventive health measure, at the beginning of each season, the grandmother would give them an infusion to "clean them out"; this would, among other benefits, rid them of the parasitic worms that were a common hazard of rural life at that time. When Vi moved up to Poughkeepsie to live with her mother, the home treatments ceased: when she had even a mild cold, her mother would take her to the doctor and he would give her medicines.

Vi's grandparents were both hard workers. For instance, in addition to her regular work, her grandmother also made quilts for all eight of the children. She would sew after breakfast and again in the afternoon. She enjoyed it, Vi says: she would use every bit of material, including the smallest scraps. Her grandmother's hands were nice, "straighter than mine," says Vi. Her grandmother would also sew clothes for the children out of the printed cotton fabric of flour sacks. On the first day of school, says Vi, she and her girl cousins would be wearing "such pretty dresses."

Her grandmother was a kind woman. Her grandfather, also kind, was stricter. When he said something, he meant it, says Vi. The kids listened to both, but waited until their grandfather was out of the house to make their special requests, because their grandmother was more likely to give them what they wanted.

Her grandfather raised all his own meat and vegetables. He built a house for them all with his own hands. She says her grandfather's hands were very bent and crooked.

The family slept on straw mattresses. Once a year her grandmother would have the children empty out the old straw and fill them with new. The kids would roll around on the newly filled mattresses to hear them crackle. The mattresses were stuffed so full that before the straw settled, the kids would keep sliding off. The pillows were stuffed with chicken feathers. Once a year, the grandmother would have the children empty out the old feathers and fill them with new feathers she had saved for the purpose.

The children were expected to do their chores without being reminded. If not, they suffered the consequences. Once, Vi says, she forgot to bring water from the spring. When her grandfather, resting from his day's work, asked for a drink, she admitted that she had forgotten, and he sent her out to fetch it, even though night had fallen.

The way to the spring led past the small burial ground where some of the family rested, and she was frightened to walk by it in the dark. The children believed that ghosts roamed around after the sun was down. She had no choice, however, and she crept past the graveyard and down the hill to the spring, filled the bucket, and then ran all the way home again. She says that by the time she was back at the house, the bucket was half empty. She never forgot that chore again.

All the children grew up to be hard workers except the youngest, she says, who was the baby of the family and spoiled, and who did nothing when she grew up but have babies of her own. And, Vi is quick to point out, this sister died at the earliest age of them all, only seventy-two.

Eventually Vi moved north to live with her mother, who had a dairy farm. She continued going to school, in a two-room schoolhouse where the boys sat on one side of the room and the girls on the other. She attended up to the tenth grade. She took piano lessons for a while, and now wishes she had gone on with them, but she was a child who needed to be "pushed," she says, and her mother did not push her, being too busy. Besides running the farm, her mother worked for a local family for thirty years, mainly cooking.

Vi was married twice. Her first husband was "no good," she says: he ran after other women. Her second husband was a good man. She wishes she had met him first. The many affectionate stories she tells about him and their life together indicate that their relationship was full of love, mutual appreciation, and good fun. "When I was a Standish," Vi will say, meaning when she was married to her first husband and bore his name. She will also express it another way: "Before I was a Harriman."

She had only one child, a daughter by her first husband, but she helped to raise her two granddaughters, who lived with her for a number of years.

Helen, too, grew up on a farm in her early childhood. Her father, soon after coming over from Sweden, acquired several hundred acres of farmland on the outskirts of a Connecticut village on an elevated plateau of land. Below, in the river valley, was a large thread-manufacturing town. He owned a small herd of cows and sold milk to neighboring families. He also raised chickens and bred the cows. He owned a team of horses for plowing, and the family used to go down the long hill into town in a wagon drawn by the two horses, who would be given a rest and a drink halfway down. Her family lived on the farm until Helen was seven, when they moved into town so that her older brother could go to the local high school.

While Helen's father worked the farm, her mother kept a kitchen garden and a poultry yard, and looked after the family. After they moved into town, Helen's father worked as custodian at the high school and later at the local college. In town, Helen's father, like Vi's grandfather, built a house with his own hands. It stood on a piece of land behind the house the family occupied. When he eventually sold both houses, her father was able to afford the larger house in which she raised her own family and lived most of her life.

Helen married when she was twenty. Her husband played the saxophone and the clarinet in a dance band. Though his first love was music, he took a job in a bank to support the family, and over the years played less and less. Helen had two children born close together, both boys, and when they were still quite small, the family moved back into what was now Helen's parents' home, a large, though plain, white house in a neighborhood of roomy Victorian houses and mature shade trees on the side of the hill overlooking the river valley and the mills. A self-contained apartment was created for them on the second and third floors. For the rest of their lives, Helen took care of her parents as well as her own family. Her mother was ill and bedridden for the last thirteen years of her life.

After her parents were both gone, the house also sheltered, for a few years following the end of World War II, a succession of displaced families from refugee camps in Germany sponsored by Helen and her husband, some of whom still send her cards in the nursing home.

Helen's sons left home and started families of their own, her husband eventually died, and Helen remained alone in the large house. For a brief time, she rented the second-floor apartment. The tenants were an elderly man and his teenage granddaughter. They left after the granddaughter became pregnant, and Helen did not rent the apartment again, but used the rooms for her sons and their families when they came to visit, and for storage. Now that Helen is gone, the house stands empty.

Employment

Both Vi and Helen began working at an early age, either helping their families or earning money outside the family.

Vi first worked outside the family at age nine, earning five cents for fetching water "for a woman." One of Vi's later jobs, with her first husband, was woodcutting: they would use a two-handled saw to cut up "pulp wood" to fill a box car, for which they would earn $500. If they "skinned the bark" off each tree, the load would earn them $600. Later, she worked as a laundress in a nursing home, and still later took jobs cleaning houses and offices.

Vi teases the girls in the office who say they are tired—they've been sitting in a chair all day!

At her current housecleaning jobs, Vi works steadily from 9:00 a.m. until 4:00 or 5:00 p.m., rarely stopping, though she will occasionally pause to talk, standing where she is, for as long as ten minutes at a stretch. When she is working she does not like to eat lunch, but she will also, usually, stop once during the day to sit down at the kitchen table and eat a piece of fruit—a banana, a pear, or an apple. If she has not had a piece of fruit by the end of the day, she will take a banana, hold it up in the air with a questioning look, and then sit down sideways at the kitchen table to peel and eat it quietly, or she will take the piece of fruit home with her. In the warm and hot weather she likes to have a tall glass of cold water with an ice cube in it. The heat does not particularly bother her, though, even on days when the mercury is in the nineties.

She works steadily, but she does not hurry. She says her grandmother taught them to take their time doing a job and to be thorough. She will, as she says, "put the night and the day on it," dusting every bar of a wooden chair and every spindle of a banister.

Vi's employers value her work and are loyal to her. After her eighty-fifth birthday party, she went down to Washington to visit her granddaughter and stayed away far longer than she had planned. She was having work done on her teeth that extended week after week. Several months went by without a word from her, her bills piled up, and the telephone company threatened to cut off her phone service. She eventually made a visit back home to pay bills and contact employers, but in all this time no one made a move to replace her. Everyone simply got along as best they could until she was back again. She has been cleaning for the same office, a law office, for thirty years.

One of her longtime employers, an elderly woman, finally entered a nursing home. She complained to Vi that the people there did not know how to make a bed properly or to bathe her. She asked Vi if she would come to the home and continue to take care of her. Vi said she would do it in a minute, but she knew that the people who worked there would not let her.

Another employer moved to Washington and asked Vi please to move there with her and continue to work for her, but Vi would not consider moving from her home and community.

Helen helped her mother, who took in laundry, by delivering and picking up the clothes. One of her mother's customers then employed Helen for a time in her own home, to sweep and serve meals. To earn pocket money, Helen would go out into the countryside, collect wildflowers, and sell them to craft hobbyists who pressed the flowers and used them to decorate trays.

Hope, who, at age 100, would be the third case in an expanded version of this study, used to bake her own bread as a child growing up on the edge of a small town in Iowa. She would sell it to her neighbors in order to pay the costs of supporting her pony. The pony was not her own, but was lent to her for the summer in exchange for the work she would do to gentle and train it.

After her children entered school, Helen took a job doing alterations at a small, family-owned women's clothing store on Main Street. She would walk down to work and walk home again. Subsequently, she worked in the city of Hartford, also as a seamstress. To go there, she took a slow local train which wound its way through woods and past cemeteries and small towns.

Helen worked for four years for the clothing shop. The owner of this business and his wife looked after their employees, became friends with many of them, and continued some friendships long after the employment had ended. Helen's working environment was, therefore, an emotionally sustaining one. After she had been in the nursing home a year, her old boss was admitted following a stroke. He lingered for a couple of weeks, and Helen would make her way slowly, with her walker, into his room to visit him. A tall, handsome man with a smooth, pale face, he lay back on his pillow staring at her with his bright eyes, but he did not know her. His wife, often there beside him, visiting, would try to remind him, but he would shake his head.

Physical Activity: Work and Play

Both Helen and Vi have had lives filled with physical activity, most consistently walking, including long-distance, and both spent significant amounts of time outdoors in the fresh air, especially as children, but also as adults. In both cases, once childhood was past, this activity principally consisted of work of one kind or another, either for themselves or for pay. But their leisure pursuits have often been active as well. Neither Vi nor Helen ever played a sport, but both danced regularly, and Vi's travels have often included a fair amount of walking.

When Vi was a child, she walked into town for errands and to attend school. Apart from her mealtimes and the hours spent in school, she was physically active the entire day, at her chores and at play—principally outdoors—with her siblings, cousins, and friends. As a young and middle-aged adult, too, she was physically active all day, her time divided between work for her own or her family's maintenance and work for pay, in both cases physical and active.

In these, her late years, Vi continues to do all her housework and yard work herself, with occasional help from family or friends if they are visiting. She will also, from time to time, clean her granddaughter's house, or a friend's house. She cooks, gardens, and rearranges her furniture. "I was always moving things," she says; "my second husband used to call me 'the moving van.'" Her second husband used to clean the kitchen when she was out working, keeping the stove and oven spotless. He would clip the hedge. Now she does it herself, but thinks she does a pretty poor job of it. Her husband also planted and tended all the rose shrubs, most of which are now gone. After a full day's work housecleaning, she will take home some plants and immediately put them in the ground. She says she likes to get her hands in the dirt.

After the working day is over, she will not only go on to tend her garden but, on certain days, leave the house after supper and spend the evening at choir practice. At a party just recently, she was one of the models in a fashion show, which required her to change into and out of eight different outfits. She admits to being tired afterward ("I was so tired, I can't tell you; my bed said to me, 'I'm waitin' for you'"). But after going to bed early that night, she rose early the next day, Sunday, baked a pan full of macaroni and cheese for the church dinner, went out and worked in the yard, worked in the house, and after resting went off to the church dinner. After the dinner, because almost everyone else had left, she stayed behind to wash the dishes with a couple of friends, also elderly. They were at the church working until midnight.

Vi washes her clothes in a washing machine but hangs them to dry on a line outdoors or in the basement, as did Helen when she lived at home; neither owns a dryer, though both could afford it. Their caregivers, as they were growing up, no doubt taught them to take advantage of a "good drying day." It should be noted that hanging clothes out and taking them in again expends considerably more energy than transferring them to a dryer, and also involves exposure to the outside air and sunlight, thus no doubt adding another small measure to Vi's and Helen's well-being.

Hope, by contrast, has avoided housework as much as possible all her adult life, having felt she had better things to do.

As Helen was growing up, she, like Vi, would walk considerable distances almost every day. When she lived outside of town, up on the farm, she walked to school, besides helping with housework and farm work and playing outdoors. When she moved into town, she continued to walk to school, a distance of seven or eight blocks each way. Her recreations as a teenager, besides dancing, included such group physical activities as scavenger hunts, then called "mystery hunts," that involved roaming the town for several hours.

When she was a young mother, she would take her small sons out into the countryside onto friends' farmland to pick berries, which she would then bake into a pie.

Helen walked wherever she needed to go. Her house was four blocks up from the main street, the last block very steep. She walked down to the shop where she worked, and walked home again. When she went into the city to work or to shop at G. Fox's department store, she would walk to and from the train station, a distance of at least six blocks. In her later years, when she no longer went down to Main Street, she would still walk half a block up the hill and then several blocks over to her church on Sunday and, unless a friend gave her a lift, back home again.

Besides this lifetime—more than eighty years—of walking up and down the long hill, there was the work in and around the house. Like Vi, Helen, when she lived in her house, did all the housework and yard work herself. In the course of her day, it was not unusual for her to go down into the basement several times to fetch something or to hang out some wet clothes, and to climb, more than once, one flight to the second floor or two flights to the attic to find a piece of clothing or put a photograph away.

Even after her eyesight went, Helen continued to look after the house without regular help, tidying and cleaning, watering the African violets on the dining-room windowsills and the Christmas cactuses upstairs in the sunny front room. The house was still perfectly neat, though not quite as clean, since she could not see that the ruffled yellow curtains in the kitchen were becoming dingy or that there were finger marks on the woodwork by the downstairs bathroom where she rested her hand going in. She worked slowly and meticulously. She had such a habit of neatness, and was so attentive, that even with her advanced macular degeneration she would find, in tidying the house after the family had departed, a single small jigsaw puzzle piece on the porch floor. She was so patient that although she could not see more than light and shadows, she would slowly peel the potatoes for dinner, feeling for the eyes with her fingertips and digging each one out with the tip of the peeler. She would gently but firmly insist on doing the dishes herself, though she would sometimes lie down and rest first.

In the yard, she would rake the leaves and pick up the sticks that dropped from the many overhanging trees; in winter, she shoveled at least some of the snow. Family would help only with the heavier jobs: a visiting son would trim the hedge, bring the porch furniture up from the basement, put on or take off storm windows. A grandchild would sometimes help with the leaves or the sticks. If there was an unusual problem she could not handle, such as squirrels in the attic, one of her sons would help. If there was an emergency, such as a fire in the chimney, she would call her next-door neighbors.

All these various activities continued until she entered the nursing home at age ninety-one.

Whereas Vi is still active, Helen now spends the better part of her day sitting in a chair by her bed. She must deliberately seek exercise: with a nursing home aide or volunteer, or a family member, she walks all the way around the nursing home, which is laid out in the shape of a diamond surrounding an open-air courtyard. Leaning on her walker, she heads off in one direction or the other, past the residents' rooms, most of them doubles, past the hairdressing salon (hours posted on the door), past the doors out to the courtyard, the front lobby and the stained-glass swinging doors into the chapel, a lounge with a large-screened television and a card table, a nurses' station, another passage leading to the courtyard, the recreation room, the residents' showers, the dining room, another nurses' station, the staff lounge with its locked door and its snack and soda machines visible through a window, another residents' lounge with a smaller television and a bookcase, the kitchen, and more residents' rooms, until she reaches her own room again. Here she parks her walker, backs up to her chair, bends to grip its arms, and sinks down into it saying "Ah" with a smile, relieved that the walk is done.

Hope, too, deliberately seeks her exercise: she takes her walker out into the long hall of her apartment building with its smell of fresh plaster; and with a friend, a family member, or her paid companion by her side, she walks a set number of times to the windowed door at the far end and back to the identical windowed door at the near end, sometimes encountering a neighbor along the way. She then returns to her apartment, lies back on her old blue sleigh bed with its litter of books and magazines, papers and notebooks, purse, tray table, and ragged cloth napkin, and rests for a moment before continuing her exercise with a set number of arm and leg lifts. When she is done, she asks for her water to be refilled; she must have water in two glasses by her bedside, one half full, next to her, the other full, at arm's length.

Present Living Situation

Helen's house is a large one, with four floors that were once in constant use: a basement for storage and laundry, a ground floor with kitchen, dining room, two parlors, a small bathroom, and Helen's bedroom; a second floor with another kitchen, a large front room, two bedrooms and a larger bathroom, and an attic floor containing one bedroom and one storeroom.

Though Vi's house is smaller than Helen's, it, too, has a basement, a ground floor, a second floor, and an attic. And like Helen's, it has a second kitchen on the second floor, part of a self-contained apartment created for rental. Three generations of a family lived there at one time: a grandfather, granddaughter, and the granddaughter's child.

Vi's house is in a pleasant, integrated neighborhood of modest but attractive and generally well-cared-for older houses that sits high above the confluence of a wide creek and an estuary, though most of the houses do not have a view of the water. Many are single-family houses, with their own well-tended yards. Many, like Vi's, are of brick, since the manufacture of bricks was once a dominant industry of the region, while some are of clapboard. Vi's house is painted white, and the eave of her enclosed front porch is lined by a black-and-white-striped metal awning. Her yard contains a small patch of lawn in front and a larger square of lawn in back by the garage. It is bordered by a low hedge along the driveway, and is ornamented by a variety of perennial plantings, including several clumps of phlox, a few hostas, and one rosebush.

Vi's house and Helen's are both clean and tidy, but whereas Helen's rooms are, some of them, remarkably empty, Vi's are crowded. One upstairs bedroom in Helen's house, for instance, contains nothing but a single bed, a folding wooden chair, and a lamp; the closet is empty, the windows curtainless, and the floor and the walls bare. Even in the reception rooms downstairs, very few decorative objects are in evidence. In the back parlor, the end tables by the sofa display only two: one a delicate Venetian glass vase brought back to her from Italy by her younger son; the other of unknown provenance and harder to classify—a teacup and saucer knitted from blue and white cotton. Every room in Vi's house, on the other hand, is filled with knickknacks, whatnot tables, easy chairs, heavy rugs and drapes, lamps, stacks of storage boxes, and vases of artificial flowers.

Whereas Vi's walls are covered with photographs and plaques awarded to her by her church, Helen has only three or four photos on display in each of her two parlors, her bedroom, and the upstairs guest room; she possesses many more, but keeps them in albums or boxes in bureau drawers. Vi has perhaps seventy to eighty photos hanging on the walls or standing on the surfaces of, particularly, her living and dining rooms. Both Vi and Helen display pictures of grandparents, parents, brothers and sisters, husbands, children, grandchildren, and friends. In addition, Vi likes to display pictures of her employers' pets, though not her employers themselves. Because one of Helen's sons is an artist, her parlor walls are hung with his paintings, the earlier ones figurative and the later ones abstract. These contrast noticeably in spirit with such odd, occasional knick-knacks as the knitted cup and saucer.

Vi's closets are packed with clothes, some of which she has not worn in years. (When she wants to describe a closet full of clothes all in a mess, she says they "walk out of the closet and say how de do!") The organizer of a recent church fashion show made a visit to Vi's house to search these closets and created a good number of outfits from them. Helen's closets, on the other hand, are spare and reduced to the essentials, containing mostly just a few simple, functional, everyday clothes: cardigans, blouses, shirtwaist dresses, skirts, and housecoats. Some of these clothes came as gifts from her family at Christmas and birthdays, but often they are clothes that she has worn for years, sometimes passed on to her long ago by a friend, her sister, or her sister-in-law. She can afford to buy new clothes, but a long habit of thrift makes her see such expenditure as rarely necessary. She seems perfectly content with what she has.

Unused clothing is stored in the spare rooms of Helen's house. In a bureau drawer in a guest room is a box containing a bed jacket or nightie that she has been given as a gift. A closet in one upstairs bedroom and a rack in the attic contain a small number of seasonal out-fits that she is not wearing at the moment. When the season changed, she used to bring these down to replace the clothes in her bedroom closet; now she asks someone else to bring the clothes to her in the nursing home. When she still lived at home, she was continually sort-ing through what she had and reducing it further. She would come down with her slight stoop and her small steps from an upstairs room or the attic carrying an item of clothing or a piece of table linen or a brooch: "Could you use this?" she would ask.

Helen's house was always tidy, because she cleaned up right away. She had a place for each thing and she put it away in its place as soon as she was finished using it. There was one exception to this practice: instead of carrying an empty cardboard box down to the cellar and putting it away immediately, she would toss it down the cellar stairs and put it away the next time she went down—in this one case valu-ing economy of motion over tidiness. Tidiness is her habit, but she does not preach it, whereas Vi readily tells a child or young person that it is important to put his or her things away in order to know where to find them again. Vi's house is so much more crowded than Helen's that it does not look as obviously tidy as Helen's.

Both Vi and Helen have mottoes on the walls of the kitchen, but Vi's tend to be purely humorous while Helen's—in Swedish, English, or both—are either religious ("God Bless This House") or sentimen-tal ("Home Sweet Home" and *"Hem kara hem"*) or moralistic (*"Den som vinner tid, vinner allt"*) or humorous with a moral message ("The hurrieder I go, the behinder I get") or simply friendly (*"Villkomen"*). Also hanging in Helen's kitchen are several pictures intended to charm or entertain, such as a photograph of a frightened kitten cling-ing by its front paws to a thin branch.

Though she goes back to visit her house from time to time, Helen now lives in a shared room in a pleasant nursing home. Her half of the room is on the hall side rather than the window side, and is there-fore darker, but she prefers not to be moved. She has had two roommates so far. The first was bedridden and mentally incompetent, emitting only groans and shouts except for the one intermittent phrase "Oh boy oh boy." This woman died after a year, and the space is now occupied by an active woman in her forties with chronic progressive dementia. She is in the early stages of the disease and currently functions very well, caring for the cats and birds that live in the nursing home and giving Helen whatever help she can, as with the telephone, with selecting food choices from the daily menu offerings, and with many other necessary tasks. Helen and she have become fond of each other, and Helen's only difficulty with her is that the roommate, whether because of her disease or her medication, talks perhaps twice as fast as the average person, so that Helen, with her impaired hearing, cannot always understand her.

Because the nursing home is located in the town in which Helen has lived all her life, she regularly discovers, among the other residents, old friends or acquaintances who are in the home either for a short rehabilitation or, more usually, for permanent care. She had not been living there long, for instance, when one of her sons read off to her the names of the two women who lived directly across the hall. To her astonishment, one was Ruth, a close friend from her childhood with whom she had lost touch. Helen immediately went across the hall to visit her friend. The woman, however, was mentally incapacitated and, though Helen spent some time talking to her and recalling events from their youth, did not recognize her. Later, Helen showed her son a photograph in which she, in the front row, and Ruth, in the second, stood among ten or twelve other girls in their white confirmation dresses and curled hair, holding flowers.

Recreation

Although Vi sings in church, she does not sing while she works, or at other times.

Helen sang in church regularly as part of the congregation. She also sang Swedish songs with her family when she was growing up. When she still lived at home, she would sometimes hum softly along with the hymns that were chimed by a nearby church every evening at six o'clock. In the nursing home, she has occasionally been induced to sing a few carols with the other residents during a Christmas sing-along. She sings tremulously and so faintly as to be almost inaudible, her expression vacant and her eyes, behind their wide bifocal lenses, directed into the vague distance.

Every evening before bedtime, however, she goes across the hall to sing a Swedish children's prayer to her old friend Ruth.

When Vi's granddaughters lived with her, she used to come home in the evening exhausted after working sometimes not just one but two jobs, and the little girls would want to teach her a new dance. "Come on, Gramma," they would say, "come on, dance with us." She would say, "No, I'm tired, I'm too tired." They would say, "Come on, Gramma, come on, dance with us—it's good exercise!" and she would give in and dance with them before she went to lie down.

Helen danced as a teenager, as often as once a week. Later, she would go to the dances where her husband was playing in the band, and still later, she and her husband would go out dancing together. When she still lived at home and her balance was good, she would occasionally catch hold of a grandchild's hands and dance with him for a moment by the kitchen door, singing a little tune to go along with the dance.

Activities with other people have been both Vi's and Helen's main forms of recreation all their lives. For Vi, most recently, these have taken the form of church activities, dinners with family or friends in her home, and travel. For Helen, they have been mostly confined to visits from family and friends and occasional scheduled events in the nursing home. Earlier in her married life, besides dancing with her husband, Helen liked to give card parties at home. She also put on regular dinners with friends and family, often including such characteristically Swedish dishes as pickled herring, pickled beets, meatballs, and limpa.

Reading was a form of recreation for Helen before her eyes went, but not for Vi. When Vi reads, it is the Bible. Helen used to read the Bible and other Christian books, such as *The Good Christian Wife*, but also magazines and the romantic novels of popular women authors like Judith Krantz.

Vi watches some television, but not much. She has a set in her kitchen that is on most of the time, especially when her daughter is visiting, but she is often busy cooking, talking on the telephone, or visiting with friends, and only intermittently pays attention to it. She is shocked by the low level of many of the programs.

At home, Helen had a console television set in the corner of her living room and used to watch game shows and one soap opera in particular, *As the World Turns*. After her eyesight became so poor, she would still listen to the programs, but then she abandoned television altogether. She also listened to the radio that she kept in the kitchen on a shelf over the sink, not only the Sunday sermons and inspirational talks, but also the women's basketball games, which she followed with some ardor: a tense moment in a game was one of the rare occasions when she was, in her own gentle way, assertive with another person, asking by the most delicate of gestures—an upraised hand and a tilt of the head—for a pause in the conversation so that she could hear the outcome of the play. She is still a fan of the UConn team. Vi does not seem to follow sports at all.

Neither Vi nor Helen is very interested in world or national news in areas such as economics, politics, literature, or art. They are both keenly interested in news of disasters and in human interest stories involving a universal theme in a particularly dramatic form—love, loss, betrayal, perversion, gross injury or disability, death. They may also, exceptionally, comment on some recent legislation that will affect them directly. But the news that engages them most is strictly local, concerning those close to them—and this includes not only their immediate friends and family but also their friends' extended family; in these areas they are quite up-to-date on the latest information, most often remembering all names and ages and relationships of those involved.

Now that Helen spends so many hours sitting in her chair by her bed, unable to read or watch television, she confides that her main leisure activity, when she is alone, is to remember and relive incidents and episodes from her past life.

Travel

Vi learned to drive at the age of sixty. Her last surviving cousin never drove a car, and it didn't do her any good, Vi says, always to be standing on street corners in all types of weather waiting for a bus or a taxi. Certain friends of Vi's will drive around town but will not drive to any other town, but Vi is not afraid to drive a fair distance.

She drives a large car that was her second husband's particular pride: he always kept it perfectly cleaned and shined. She says he would be so ashamed to see how she takes care of it, although it looks fairly clean and tidy to anyone else. True, she does allow dust to gather on the dashboard and tiny scraps of litter on the floor.

The fact that Helen never drove a car meant that in later life she and two of her friends shared their weekly trip out for groceries; thus, the necessary chore became a pleasant social occasion.

Vi travels regularly within the country and occasionally out of the country, whereas Helen no longer travels and rarely did.

Vi goes to Washington to visit her granddaughter, and sometimes farther south to attend a wedding or funeral. She either drives with her daughter or takes the bus with a friend. Other, local trips are either by car, when she drives herself, or in the church van, when the choir is going off somewhere to sing.

Helen has traveled very little in her life, though members of her extended family have gone to Sweden to visit historical family sites. She took several vacations in New England with her husband and sons and, after she was widowed, two trips to Florida with her brother. In all of her life, she has lived away from her hometown only once: after she graduated from high school, her brother drove her down to New York City, where she settled in Brooklyn and studied dressmaking for one year at the Pratt Institute. After she was married and raising her two sons, she rarely went farther from home than to Hartford by train.

For many years now, travel for Helen has been limited to drives around town and into the countryside as a passenger. She looks out the window, and despite her near-blindness manages to identify old landmarks from her younger years: a friend's farm, the group home where her friend Robert lives with his large collection of first-edition books, the house where she once worked as a maid, her friends' florist shop, the house on Oak Street where her family first lived after they left the farm, and the house in back of it that her father built.

Pets and Other Animals

Both Helen and Vi are very fond of animals and have had pets and domestic animals in their lives from early childhood.

Vi is more partial to dogs; she has more stories about them, and photographs of them. But she is also amused by cats, especially one small black cat that tries to grab the dust cloth out of her hand where she works—helping her to clean, she says. Her backyard is full of strays and neighborhood cats, though she does not feed them. The old woman next door feeds them, she says, and although some of the other neighbors object, Vi sees no harm in it, since this is one of the old woman's few pleasures and she will be gone from this world soon enough. When Vi talks about this old woman, she seems to forget that she herself, being eighty-five, is also an old woman.

In Helen's early life, there were the two horses, as well as the cows, calves, cats and kittens, and a large flock of chickens. In her adult life, she has almost always had a cat as a pet. She used to feed strays at her back door, and one winter arranged a cardboard box

shelter for one of them under the outside staircase. She would walk
out over the ice with small, careful steps just before dark to set his
evening meal down in the snow. There are cats in the nursing home,
and one in particular, a large Persian, will occasionally wander in to
visit her. She speaks to him, smiles, and reaches her hand down to
him, though in her eyes he is only an orange blur.

*Hope kept an overweight female cat throughout her later years, with some-
times harmony between them and sometimes ill will. She was sure the cat
harbored resentments and indulged in some calculated bad behavior. When,
eventually, she was advised by a home health expert that the cat posed a certain
hazard to her by crouching in dark corners, getting underfoot, and occasionally attacking her ankles, she immediately arranged for it to be put down by the
local vet before her family could intervene.*

Although Helen, when she lived at home, kept a bird feeder well
supplied outside the kitchen window where she could watch it over
her morning coffee, she had no great love of, or interest in, other
sorts of wild creatures.

Vi, the same in this respect, particularly dislikes snakes and often
repeats a long story about finding one in her yard and going after it
with a shovel. When she was a child in Virginia, the windows were
kept open in the summertime and lizards would climb up to sun
themselves on the windowsills. The children were scared of the
lizards and wanted to kill them. But Vi's grandmother told them the
lizards would not hurt them, to let the lizards stay there and enjoy
the sun, and they would go away when they were ready.

Neither Helen nor Vi is particularly interested in the natural
world beyond the confines of the garden. Nature for Helen, when she
still lived at home, manifested itself either as a practical problem—
trees shading the house, the lawn that did not grow well, the hedge
that needed clipping, acorns in the driveway—or a domesticated
thing of beauty like her favorite, the azalea shrub, or the dogwood in
blossom. Her work in the yard was caretaking work rather than
designing and planting, with the exception of the geraniums, which

she liked to see set out in the spring in a row by the front porch. Every spring, too, she looked for the first blooms of the flowering bulbs.

She also enjoyed nature in the form of the landscape as seen from the car window on a Sunday drive.

Religion

Both Helen and Vi have maintained close involvement with their churches all their lives, although the church has loomed larger in Vi's life than in Helen's. Their churches have constituted their most important larger community, both social and spiritual.

In youth and middle age, Helen participated in the church's ladies' auxiliary group and helped out with such projects as bake sales for fund-raising. Every summer her family attended the church picnics. She said grace before every meal while she still lived at home. It is important to her that every family member be baptized, although her gentle insistence about this has sometimes had no effect. Her religious beliefs do not explicitly enter or color her conversation. She now rarely goes to a church service because the chapel in her nursing home is Catholic.

Vi's strong faith occasionally enters her conversation, when she refers to "God's will" or, more jocularly, describes what God might have in mind for her future. When she used to visit the local prison, she would incorporate some Christian teaching in her conversations with the prisoners. She likes to spend time at Bible study with her best friend on a warm Saturday evening in summer. They take chairs out into the backyard, and as it grows dark they read aloud to each other from Scripture, discussing each passage in preparation for the following day's Bible class.

Hope reacted against her mother's strong religious convictions by rejecting all organized religions and in fact all forms of spirituality, as well as, though indirectly, by joining, at one stage, the Communist Party.

Vi spends most of every weekend on church activities. She was for a time president of an official churchwomen's group, the Deaconesses. She sings in the choir, which involves going to choir rehearsals as well as occasionally traveling to other churches, often in distant towns, to give performances. Congregations of different churches also visit each other: often her church will visit another for a supper, or her church will prepare a supper to host another church, when she will bake and help wash up afterward. She will exclaim later over the quantity of food consumed by the other congregation.

In her walk around the nursing home, Helen will sometimes ask family members to look for the names of acquaintances. She will always stop in front of the chapel. Here, next to the open stained-glass doors, a signboard with a black background and removable white letters bears the names of those residents who are in the hospital or recently deceased and in need of a candle and/or a prayer. She will ask to have the names read to her in case they include someone she knows.

Personal Habits

Both Vi's and Helen's eating habits are sensible, Vi's diet marginally more balanced since she includes more fresh fruits and vegetables. Neither is particularly health-conscious; their good habits are also the habits of their families of origin.

Both have always practiced moderation, eaten regular meals, and enjoyed food and the preparation of food, although Vi has been more explicitly enthusiastic about food than Helen. Both have eaten predominantly home cooking (including baking) all their lives, and although they enjoy restaurant meals have tended to eat very little food that could be called convenience, junk, or fast food, with the exception of sandwiches and pastries. When they were children, of course, neither one ever ate in a restaurant.

When Vi was growing up on the farm in Virginia, the family ate their own fruits and vegetables—fresh in season and home-canned in winter—and the animals they raised themselves. They bought almost nothing but sugar in a sack, which the children would carry home—and on the way, Vi says, being mischievous and fun-loving, they would sneak a taste by sucking a corner of the sack.

In contrast to her light lunch when she is working at a cleaning job, Vi has a hearty breakfast and dinner. For breakfast she has a glass of milk, a glass of juice, cereal, eggs, bacon, and toast. With her second husband she used to have pancakes on Sundays, with coffee. She drinks quite a lot of milk now, but did not when she was younger. When she goes home after a day of work, she says, she makes herself a nice dinner. In the cold weather she likes to start with a bowl of soup. "A little bowl?" "No, a medium-sized bowl." Then she has some meat, perhaps meatballs, pork chops, or chicken and vegetables. She makes the soup and the meatballs herself. She likes her own cooking. She does not care for meat now, though, as much as she used to; she likes vegetables and fruit more.

Helen used to order a Reuben sandwich when she went out to lunch: corned beef and cheese on rye bread. She would, however, eat only half the sandwich, taking the other half home for her next day's lunch. She liked to go out for doughnuts after church with her friends. They would also have breakfast together in a restaurant every Wednesday, before they did their grocery shopping. In her later years, her cupboards used to contain a good deal of canned food as well as Lipton tea, Sanka, boxes of pastries and cookies, and spices, flour, and sugar for baking. She liked sweets, but ate them in small quantities. She would have a piece of fruit during the day. She would buy prepared seafood salad for sandwiches. For family dinners, she regularly made mashed potatoes and what she called a "salad," which consisted of an aspic mold containing grated carrots, Jell-O, and pineapple. Earlier in her life, she would bake pastries and breads for her family, setting the dough to rise on the radiators in winter.

Both Vi and Helen like rhubarb and welcome a chance to have it fresh out of a friend's or family's garden and eat it stewed. Vi bends down herself and gives each stalk a vigorous twist at the base to break it off, collecting half a dozen to take home with her. In Helen's case, her family brings it to her already stewed and ready to eat, but there is always the danger that a member of the nursing home staff will remove the tub of slimy-looking fruit and throw it out, as happened once, before Helen has a chance to enjoy it.

Hope has been adamant, all her life, in planning a healthy food program for herself. Now, every day, under her instruction, her live-in companion prepares for her, for lunch, a bean soup, a small salad, and a small bowl of popcorn, followed by a fruit and yogurt dessert. She sometimes calls out to her companion several times to see if lunch is ready yet or to request additional services that delay the preparation of the meal. When the time comes, she makes her way slowly to the dining area via the kitchen, where she may give a few more instructions. While she eats, she wears a cracked green plastic tennis visor over her eyes to shade them from the overhead chandelier and watches a book program on the television.

Neither Helen nor Vi ever smoked. When she was small, Vi and her cousin Joe had tried smoking their grandmother's pipe when she was away. There wasn't much tobacco in it, but Vi became very sick. Later, she didn't dare tell her grandmother why she was so sick. If her grandparents had found out what she had done, she says, "I woulda had some sores *now*" from it. This bad experience discouraged her from ever wanting to smoke again.

Hope had the occasional cigarette in her twenties, during the years when, stylish and attractive, she also tended to form various short-lived attachments to, often, wealthy and well-born lovers and traveled abroad, sometimes at their expense. However, smoking did not agree with her and she did not continue.

Vi does not habitually drink alcohol at all. She says she likes her Manishevitz, but the last time she drank any, in fact, was many years ago: an employer used to invite her to breakfast and offer her a small glass, but that employer is long gone. Helen, before she moved into the nursing home, would occasionally be persuaded to have a little

161

sweet wine after a holiday meal: seated in her customary place at one end of the dining table, in front of a glass-fronted cupboard containing sets of delicate sherry glasses and some commemoration plates and mugs, she would sip it slowly and thoughtfully. Now she does not have wine or any other alcohol.

Hope, by contrast, has drunk wine and mixed drinks all her life, enjoying an altered state of mind in which she is more apt to make risqué or tactless remarks, and whether or not company is present, she often has a glass of wine with her dinner.

For guests, she likes to open a bottle of champagne: When they arrive at the door, she is immediately distracted by the thought of the champagne and barely greets them before sending them to find it in the refrigerator. After the champagne has been drunk, she will sometimes have her guests bring out a leftover bottle of wine from the refrigerator, though it is ice-cold and may be sour.

Both Helen and Vi are thrifty by habit. Vi's second husband would look out for sales and buy, for instance, ten large bottles of bleach for thirty-nine cents a bottle. Vi, too, buys in quantity. She keeps these extra supplies on her small enclosed side porch.

Helen has a metal serving spoon which she used to stir things on the stove for so long that it is worn down nearly straight on one side.

When her daughter was a child, Vi was given nice hand-me-down children's clothes, including party dresses, by her employers. She would pack them carefully away until her daughter was the right size for them, then wrap them festively and present them for birthdays and Christmases as though they were new. Her daughter never suspected. Now Vi's daughter in turn brings her good clothing from yard sales. Vi rarely buys a piece of new clothing for herself.

Vi does not buy more food than she needs, and she does not let it spoil. The same was true of Helen when she lived at home and cooked for herself. Vi drinks Lipton tea, and she uses each teabag twice, sometimes three times.

Helen, by now, in the restricted space of the nursing home, feels somewhat oppressed and burdened by her possessions, though she has so few. More inclined to give than receive, she resists offers of presents, though she sometimes appears secretly pleased by them; "No, no," she will say gently, "don't bring me anything. I don't need *anything*!" Sometimes, only, she may ask for a bag of cough drops or a bar of soap.

Vi is quite open about liking to receive presents. She appreciates framed photographs, plants, and boxes of chocolates. At the end of her day's work, she likes to take home, in the growing season, either produce from an employer's vegetable patch or a perennial plant dug up out of the ground. But she likes gifts of money more than anything else. On the occasion of her eighty-fifth birthday, not only her employers but most of her friends gave her money.

Whether in order to make an economical choice or, more likely, to save trouble for her family, Helen, some years ago, went with her older son to a local funeral parlor, chose a casket, and paid in advance for the casket and funeral arrangements. With the same foresight, she had already chosen the nursing home in which she now lives.

Health

Vi is rarely ill, having only the occasional cold in her head and chest. She has some arthritis in her left shoulder, which prevents her raising her left arm above shoulder height. She has to compensate when working by using her other arm for some things. For a time she was given physical therapy for it, but it didn't get much better. She believes, though, that if you have arthritis, you have to use the affected limb, otherwise it will get worse and worse. She will cite the examples of several friends who moved less and less until they could not move at all. She has no other physical problems and takes no medication.

Although Helen's eyesight and hearing are poor, she takes no prescription medications, her only pills being vitamins and an occasional aspirin. She had no medical problems until the age of eighty, when she began to develop macular degeneration, which has grown progressively worse. Sometime after she turned ninety, a friend of hers noticed, on their weekly grocery shopping trip, that her ankles were badly swollen. Helen went to the doctor and it was discovered that her heart had begun to beat more slowly and erratically. She was fitted with a pacemaker. Following insertion of the pacemaker, medical problems began that appeared to have been caused by the medical interventions themselves. For instance, a heart medication upset her stomach. This in turn caused her to lose weight and weaken, making her more prone to falling. One fall resulted in a broken hip. She entered her present nursing home on a temporary basis for treatment and then arranged to stay there permanently. In the nursing home, a treatment with a medicated shampoo led to a chronic and persistent skin irritation that she will apparently never be free of. Two of her medical problems, then—her macular degeneration and her erratic heartbeat—occurred naturally and spontaneously, whereas the others—the weight loss with resultant weakness, the fall and fracture, and the skin condition—resulted from medical intervention.

Helen's well-being is dependent, now, on the environment of the nursing home and the treatment she receives there.

Physical Appearance

Both Helen and Vi take pride in their appearance. Both, *like Hope*, were attractive and popular with boys and men when they were younger. Their figures are strong, slender, and youthful. They have smooth, clear skin, Helen's pale but with a diffused rosy color and Vi's a rich, even brown.

Vi's face is round, her eyes are dark brown and sparkling and slant upward a little at the outer edges. Her eyebrows are straight and thick. Her lips are often parted, as though she is about to speak or smile, and then her lower lip curves downward. Helen's blue eyes are dim now, the whites yellowish. Both Helen and Vi wear large glasses, though Vi often removes hers for a photograph. Vi's hands are shapely and dark brown. Her fingers are slim and fairly straight; only the last joint of the index finger is a little bent and swollen. Helen's fingers are quite crooked.

A photograph of Helen taken when she was about twenty years old shows her leaning against the front porch of the large white house, her hands behind her back. Her head is tilted to one side, and she is smiling. Her black dress is low-waisted, with a V neck, a loosely knotted black tie at the V, and a flared, pleated, knee-length skirt. She wears clear stockings and black heeled pumps with ankle straps. She has a string of pearls around her neck. Her long, dark hair is parted and tied back.

Both Vi and Helen pay attention to their clothes and enjoy dressing nicely. As a teenager, Vi wore a variety of handsome, but conservative, tailored clothes—blouses, suits, coats—of interesting fabrics, with detailed buttons and belts. She is pictured in one photograph wearing a wide-lapeled camel coat, a black beret, and a black scarf. In another, she is shown with a much older boyfriend who appears to be in his thirties and is dressed in a double-breasted suit, bi-colored handkerchief folded into a triangle in his breast pocket, a tie with tiepin, and a hat, a cigar clamped in his mouth—but, as Vi points out, his pants have no crease. Here, she is wearing a pale blue dress with white buttons and a round white collar under a dark coat with a small white fur collar, and lavender heeled pumps with straps. In another photograph, with another boyfriend, this one her own age, she is wearing a dress with full cream-colored blouse and sleeves and broad swathes of lace down the front and around the neck. Her hair is simply arranged with a part down the middle, she is wearing her glasses, and, as in all her photographs, she has a relaxed, happy smile.

For a house-cleaning job, Vi often goes out dressed in clean and pressed blue jeans, sneakers, and a sweatshirt or a sweater or, in warm weather, a T-shirt. Dressed in this way, she appears as athletic as a young girl. Very rarely, her head is wrapped in a kerchief tied in back; more usually, she is bareheaded, her hair braided in one of a variety of different styles. Her hair is still mostly dark, with only a little gray in it. When she dresses up for a party or church function, however, she wears a wig of smooth, waved, and styled black hair streaked with silver and a fancy dress of shiny material, sometimes with bouffant sleeves and a wide skirt, sometimes more streamlined. The change in her appearance is startling: she looks younger than her age, but also more formal, losing her youthful or tomboyish vivaciousness. In this guise she is known to most of the other church members not as Vi or Viola but as Mother Harriman.

When Helen still lived at home, she would have breakfast—often just a piece of toast and a cup of instant coffee—in her nightgown, housecoat, and slippers. Then, after washing the breakfast dishes, she would wash herself and dress in stockings, low-heeled pumps, a skirt, a blouse with a pin, or a dress, and sometimes a cardigan. She was always well groomed and her colors were pleasing in combination, if muted. Her gray hair was styled in a permanent wave. When she moved into the nursing home she immediately abandoned the permanent wave, and now her hair is straight and cut fairly short, a shiny silver, usually pinned to the side with a bobby pin. She now wears knee socks instead of stockings, and athletic shoes because they have good support and traction.

Both Vi and Helen are graceful. They stand and move in an economical, balanced way, Helen more slowly and deliberately now than Vi. Neither one has ever been awkward, clumsy, or hasty. They know the importance of not rushing. If an employer or a friend has to go out on an errand, Vi will say, with a pleasant lilt to her words, "Take your time!"

Helen has always thought and planned ahead, and has been prepared for what she will do next. This is one of the reasons she is not clumsy and does not hurry. Only once did her younger son ever see her moving fast, and that was during an emergency: a little girl had fallen into a neighbor's well and was drowning.

Vi's posture is fully upright; she stands poised and balanced on her feet with her shoulders back and her head up, facing the person she is talking to and looking him or her directly in the eye. Helen has a slight stoop in her back and shoulders, and when she is seated, she tends to be rather graciously inclined toward the person she is talking to, this tendency no doubt exacerbated by her weak hearing. While she still lived in her own house, this forward inclination, as she peeled a potato or climbed the stairs with something in her arms, was expressive of her general state of readiness and activity, and even of her generosity, as she reached out a crooked hand to touch a grandchild or show a photograph.

Personality and Temperament

Both Vi and Helen are polite and gracious in their actions and responses, and appreciative and thoughtful of others. But beyond these good manners, both have a good deal of personal charm. This expresses itself in their voices, facial expressions, bearing, wit, and alertness of response. They maintain steady eye contact; their expressions are relaxed and smiling, their voices are well inflected, rising and falling pleasantly; they are closely attentive to the conversation in progress and quick to respond with a thoughtful remark.

Both Vi and Helen are so friendly and charming that they consistently elicit positive reactions from others—their friends, employers, doctors, nurses, church congregation members, children and grandchildren—and therefore in turn receive, from these others, the sustenance of friendliness, consideration, and wit.

At present, although, inevitably, certain of the staff at the nursing home are by nature unresponsive, cold in manner, or bad-tempered, most have become very fond of Helen and describe her modest and generous personality either directly—"She'll never tell you if she needs something"—or with gentle irony: "Oh, Helen— she's such a complainer!"

Vi appears to be happy, at times exuberant, often vivacious. By contrast, Helen is more subdued. Perhaps because of her infirmities and her permanent residence in the nursing home, she sometimes indicates quite directly, though with a resigned smile, that she will not mind when the time comes for her to die, or even that she will welcome it. If Vi, on the other hand, mentions her own "passing," it is in a humorous context.

Both rebound from difficulties, Vi often seeing the lighter side of a situation, Helen tending to accept the inevitable—"Well," she will say with a shrug and a smile, "what can you do?"

Both display enthusiasm, though Vi's is more vocal and louder than Helen's. If Helen enjoys competitive sports on the radio, Vi enjoys a good meal, a good story, and even a new broom.

Both abide firmly by their long-established habits and are reluctant or unwilling to try a novel way of doing something, or even to hear about it.

Hope, by contrast, still as mentally sharp as she ever has been, appreciates any form of ingenuity, especially her own. She will report her bold ideas and her clever solutions to practical problems with a relish that she expects to be shared.

Both Helen and Vi will express disapproval of certain things, such as the manners, behavior, or work ethic of young people, but Helen will often, after a brief pause, gently append some remark indicating understanding, such as "They do their best," or "They try," whereas Vi will not soften her criticism. Helen does not like most of the changes that have occurred in her hometown over the years, such as the intrusion of a gaudy Chinese restaurant on Main Street or the closing of the old movie theater and the YMCA. Both marvel— disapprovingly—over excessive weight in others. Along with such disapproval comes a certain degree of self-approbation in both. Vi will boast outright, with a chuckle of pleasure, and tell stories to her credit, such as how she outwalked all the other church members on a recent trip to Jerusalem. Helen will not boast, but will occasionally imply, by her mild criticism, that her own way is a better way.

Both Helen and Vi give generously to their friends and family, materially and in time and attention. When Helen still lived at home, she kept boxes of cookies and pastries on a lower shelf of a dish cupboard in the kitchen; when family or friends were leaving, she would take a selection or a whole box out of the cupboard and urge it on the departing travelers. She does the same now in the nursing home. Visitors have brought her so many gift boxes of cookies, candies, and fruit that she has a large store of them in her bedside cabinet. "Would you like these ginger cookies?" she will ask. "Take this banana," she will say.

Helen calls friends regularly to see how they are. She shows her concern and interest in the questions she asks her visitors. She remembers the names of all their family members and asks after these family members, too. When she still lived at home and had the use of her eyes, she would send a card on each birthday or anniversary. For a child, she would often enclose money. She would always telephone some hours after a visit to make sure her family had gotten home safely.

In those days, Helen's form of giving was in service as well as in conversation. Besides her church activities, she would visit friends in the hospital and in nursing homes. When she still could, she would walk many blocks from her house to the rather grim nursing home where various women she knew, including her sister-in-law and her old English teacher, were living out their days. When she could no longer walk the distance, she found a ride with a friend. She often came as a visitor to the same nursing home where she is now a resident.

If a friend of Vi's is in the hospital for an extended time, she will go over to her house and clean it for her. If a friend does not drive, Vi will drive her where she needs to go. When there is a death in the family of one of Vi's friends, relatives often come from far away, usually the South, but also the Midwest and the West Coast, to attend the funeral; Vi thinks nothing of accommodating these travelers for several days, giving them beds and meals. She will report this activity and how busy she has been, commenting, "I don't know my head from my heels!" or "I been jumpin'!"

In addition to her work for the church and for friends, Vi used to pay regular visits to inmates of a local prison. There she would, in particular, scold one young man whose family she knew: "Your mother died without ever seeing you any better than you are now," she would tell him. "How could you do that to your mother? Aren't you shamed?"

Conversational Manner

Helen is more of a listener, Vi more of a talker. Vi is quite willing to express strong opinions about how things ought to be and how people ought to behave, whereas Helen is less prescriptive or assertive. Sometimes, only, she will be gently insistent when the subject is one she feels strongly about, such as baptism.

Helen answers questions about herself in just a few words and reluctantly or hesitantly, only occasionally volunteering some memory she likes to recall. She does not talk at length about herself, but she will recall the past in brief increments, as, on an outing in the car: "We used to come down this hill in a wagon with Kate and Fanny pulling it." Or she will comment wistfully on her present situation: "I haven't been shopping in so long . . .   I miss some of it."

Vi and Helen are both likely to ask questions in a conversation, but sparingly, and Helen more than Vi. Helen asks for news and listens attentively. Her questions are general inquiries, such as "How are the cats?" or "Are you going to stay home for a while now?"

Vi tends to do most of the talking, but if the person she is talking to makes a remark, she will respond with "Is that so?" or "Is that right?" with mild surprise and sudden seriousness that is sometimes genuine and sometimes merely polite. Sometimes her questions are more specific, as in "Oh, is he moving?" or "How old is he now?" but her intention is never to draw the other out at any great length. Both Helen and Vi are reserved about probing very deeply into another person's life or opinions, no doubt restrained by courtesy rather than lack of interest.

Hope, by contrast, has no reserve in this area, and asks detailed questions about even the most personal subjects. She enjoys fostering a degree of dependence in her family and friends and has no doubt about the powerful influence of her opinions and advice.

Vi often enjoys good times with her friends, and she likes to report the funny things that happen to them. She says, over and over: "Oh, I had some fun with them about that," or "Oh, we laughed a lot."

She is more interested in her own stories than those of the person she is talking to. Almost everything that has happened to her in her life can be turned into a funny story. The humor in these stories is mild, having to do with the foibles of human and animal behaviors and interactions. For instance, Vi's best friend hated dogs. This woman told the woman she worked for at her cleaning job that she wouldn't work there anymore if the employer got a dog. The employer thought Vi's friend didn't mean it, because she had worked for her so long, but she did mean it, and when the employer got a dog, Vi's friend said, "You won't be seeing any more of *me*!" and never returned. Vi's facial expressions and intonations enliven the story as she tells it, and she laughs at the end.

However difficult the situation, for Vi there is always a funny side to it. Her husband was ill in the hospital; she had just come from her night job to see him; when she left him she would have to walk two or three miles through the darkened city to get home. But the doctor said something that made her laugh and it is part of a funny story she tells. Another time, her best friend collapsed on the living-room floor at three in the morning and Vi was summoned by the family. Although they were all terrified, Vi laughs as she describes how she was down on the floor trying to help her friend when the firemen came, and what a time they had getting her out of the way so they could do their work. "Oh, it was funny." A patient in a nursing home where she worked refused to let Vi touch him because of her black skin; her sister, who also worked there, calmly advised her to ignore the insult and leave him alone, because some people were like that; but when the patient, one day, insulted Vi's sister in the same terms, Vi said, her sister was so mad she was ready to "slug" him! Oh, it was funny.

Helen does not tell stories the way Vi does, but she relays news of family, friends, and the families of friends that make up a longer ongoing story, and this story is deeply absorbing to her. Her group of friends is shrinking year by year, as those her own age die, but a good number still visit her regularly in the nursing home, or send cards on her birthday and at Christmas, and their children, too, remain in touch.

Helen speaks Standard English that includes certain regional or ethnic expressions such as "come to find out," meaning "then we found out," and "Lebanon way," meaning "in the vicinity of Lebanon"; to her, a window shade is a "curtain," and sometimes, a magazine is a "book"; she will use slang expressions such as "a live wire" and sometimes include a colorful, incongruous metaphor in her conversation, as when she remarks, apropos of how many of her friends are gone, that she is "the last of the Mohicans—as they say." She will punctuate her conversation with phrases or remarks expressive of resignation, such as "Well, anyway . . ." and "I've lived a pretty long life as it is . . ." She knows a little Swedish, from having grown up with Swedish-speaking parents and relatives. She says that just recently she suddenly recalled a Swedish prayer she had said as a child; after years in which she had not remembered it, it came back into her mind complete and intact.

Vi speaks a mixture of Standard English and her own variety of Standard Black English (sometimes she will say "he doesn't" and sometimes "he don't") sprinkled with Southern idioms ("white as cotton," "burying ground" for cemetery), old-time rural locutions ("grease" for hand lotion), and unusual, perhaps unique expressions acquired from her grandparents, particularly her grandmother, who may have made some of them up ("We had a bamboo time!"). In any single conversation, at least one or two rare, vivid phrases will occur. She is aware of how interesting these expressions are and enjoys using them. As a natural storyteller, she relishes the effect not only of the plots of her stories but also of the language she uses in telling them.

Conclusion

Although genetic inheritance surely plays a part in an individual's health and longevity, it is not unreasonable to conclude that certain shared traits in Vi's and Helen's life histories, personalities, and habits have been conducive to their longevity and good health.

Their eating habits have probably been an important factor, although, since Helen's diet has been fair but not optimal for many years, we may postulate that the fresh and unadulterated produce and animal protein of her early years on the farm established her good health and that the lifelong moderation and regularity of her meals thereafter were more important than what she actually ate. Alternatively, we may conclude that in Helen's case, eating habits may have been less important than her vigorous and constant exercise and the other factors contributing to her well-being.

Vigorous physical exercise initiated in childhood would establish good development of heart, lungs, and other muscles early in life. Exercise outdoors, earlier in the twentieth century, when air quality was better than it is now, would have provided excellent oxygenation of Vi's and Helen's developing bodies. *Hope, too, was physically active as a child, racing her ponies, canoeing with the Girl Scouts, and, as shortstop and captain, leading her softball team to victory in high school.* The fact that their figures were slender reduced stress on their bones and inner organs, and made them more likely to remain active, which in turn kept them slender. There is no doubt that abstinence from smoking and drinking alcohol would be likely to reduce stress on their livers and lungs, and promote good oxygenation of their bodily tissues.

Regular lifelong physical exercise would also act to relieve psychological stress, which would help to explain the lack of tension in both Helen and Vi; and this lack of tension would surely also be conducive to good health and longevity. Physical exercise in general would be helpful, but especially helpful would be the particular exercise provided by dancing, since it is rhythmical, cardiovascular, communal, and emotionally expressive.

Although it is harder to measure the effects of pride in their appearance; enjoyment of life, especially friends, family, food, work, and leisure activities; contentment with, or acceptance of, their situations; curiosity about the news of their friends and family; uncomplaining, cheerful temperaments; optimism; and a capacity for enthusiasm and amazement, a positive outlook may be assumed to promote a sense of well-being, good health, and, in turn, a longer life.

The sense of humor which they share so generously with others, Vi's ready laughter and Helen's gentle smile, no doubt provides another form of release, both physical and emotional, along with a strengthening of their supportive community, while their storytelling, however abbreviated in Helen's case, reinforces their firm sense of identity.

The loving, but strict, upbringing by their families of origin, with its strongly inculcated work ethic, would provide at least three major benefits: a steady emotional support, a reinforcement of identity, and training in the self-discipline that would encourage Vi and Helen to maintain good habits and find satisfaction in industry. Their close involvement with their families of origin would in turn encourage them to form close ties within their own created families and their circles of friends, these in turn providing a steady support for them. It may also be argued that the habit of orderliness which was taught them as children would be conducive to their creating and maintaining a healthy environment and thus to lessening the likelihood of their suffering a disabling or fatal accident.

Their close involvement with their church communities yields a complex of benefits, arising not only from the rituals and spiritual beliefs of the church but also from the social activities surrounding them.

Lastly, a love of domestic animals involves an interaction with a positively disposed or needy creature that generally reciprocates one's affection and provides yet another form of release from stress.

Many of the positive elements in Vi's and Helen's lives are, of course, part of a reciprocal pattern: for instance, the work Vi and Helen have done, whether at home or on a job, has provided them with a positive sense of satisfaction; or their generosity toward another person has yielded generosity in return; or their kindness to a pet has inspired affection on the part of the pet. The positive effects of their actions induce them, in turn, to repeat the actions; in other words, a positively reinforcing cycle is created that constantly perpetuates the well-being of the initiator, Vi or Helen.

November 2002

Update: In the four years since this study was written, there have been some relatively minor changes in the situations of Vi and Helen, now respectively eighty-nine and ninety-six, but their health and vitality remain very much the same.

Helen's house was sold and its contents dispersed. This meant that she could no longer ask her family to bring her something from home, for instance some piece of clothing from a certain closet. Most of her clothing was given away, as were her furniture, books, kitchenware, and linens. She did not want to move anything into the nursing home because of the lack of space. She consented only to have a single oil painting from the house to hang above her chair. It is a very early one by her son that depicts her Bible lying open on a table by a window next to a potted geranium.

The selling of the house also meant that she could no longer go back and visit it, as she used to do on excursions from the nursing home. Now her family drives past it on their way to see her, and reports to her on its condition: the new owners have rebuilt the front porch; the plantings have not changed; yesterday there was a car in the driveway; today there was a Christmas tree upstairs.

Vi now has two more great-grandchildren, or a total of four. The older ones tell the little ones they must mind her because she "belongs to the old school," as she reports with delight. Her house was badly flooded one winter when the pipes burst while she was away. It had to be completely gutted, and while Vi was waiting for the insurance company to come forward with more money for the repair work, she lived either with her granddaughter in Washington or with her best friend down the hill from her house—the same friend with whom she had studied the Bible on Saturday evenings and who had had a frightening attack at three in the morning.

When surprised by a visit at ten in the morning a year or so ago, the two companionable women, both in their eighties but looking twenty years younger, were still in their immaculately clean house robes, one hanging out a load of wash in the sunshine on a square laundry tree in the backyard and the other sitting at the gleaming Formica table in the kitchen. Vi had no immediate plans to go back to work, but also no plans to give notice to any of her employers. Later, she quit her office-cleaning job, but she does continue, though now eighty-nine years old, to clean house for at least two families.

Vi is still in good health, and active in church. She has recently taken a much-anticipated trip to Alaska which was not as successful as it might have been, since one member of the group had to go home halfway through due to a death in the family. "They never should have told her," Vi says.

Helen's health, too, is reasonably good. Now ninety-six, she takes only one prescription medication, for high blood pressure. Her balance has worsened, and her hearing has deteriorated slightly. But she is mentally alert, with an excellent memory, and her sense of humor is still lively, as is her interest in the activities of her family and friends. After several years of a successful companionship, Helen's young roommate was removed to another facility. The roommate who succeeded her was an old woman of a sour temperament, active enough to propel herself around in a wheelchair, but a constant grumbler. She died not long after arriving; Helen did not know the cause. The current roommate is a kindly Ukrainian woman with a large circle of friends and family: Helen mentions the noise produced by the long, frequent visits, though she does not explicitly complain.

Helen maintains the same rather limited physical activity as when she entered the nursing home. Since she has fallen several times, however, she is no longer allowed to move about on her own but is connected to an alarm on the back of her chair by a wire clipped to the shoulder of her blouse; the alarm will sound if she stands up. She still takes a daily walk around the nursing home when there is a volunteer or family member available to accompany her. She moves at a fairly brisk pace, leaning forward on her walker, and quietly nods or says hello to almost everyone she meets, though many residents are unaware of the meaning of her greeting and respond with a blank stare—which of course she can't see. One section of the hallway, near the entrance lobby, displays greatly enlarged framed vintage photographs, in color, of features of the town as it used to be, such as the footbridge over the river, the old shopping street with its awnings and horse-drawn carriages, the great limestone buildings of the thread mill, and the legendary frog pond of Revolutionary War fame. She calls this part of the walk "going down Main Street" and likes to stop in front of each photograph and ask questions about it. She is still reluctant to join in any of the planned activities of the home, but she will, if pressed by family members, attend a Christmas concert or "Piano with Bob" in the Recreation Room, politely staying until the very end of what may be a tedious hour-long performance.

January 2006

Reducing Expenses

This is a problem you might have someday. It's the problem of a couple I know. He's a doctor, I'm not sure what she does. I don't actually know them very well. In fact, I don't know them anymore. This was years ago. I was bothered by a bulldozer coming and going next door, so I found out what was happening. Their problem was that their fire insurance was very expensive. They wanted to try to lower the insurance premiums. That was a good idea. You don't want any of your regular payments to be too high, or higher than they have to be. For example, you don't want to buy a property with very high taxes, since there will be nothing you can do to lower them and you will always have to pay them. I try to keep that in mind. You could understand this couple's problem even if you didn't have high fire insurance. If you did not have exactly the same problem, some-day you might have a similar problem, of regular payments that were going to be too high. Their insurance was high because they owned a large collection of very good wine. The problem was not so much the collection per se but where they were keeping it. They had, actu-ally, thousands of bottles of very good and excellent wine. They were

178

keeping it in their cellar, which was certainly the right thing to do. They had an actual wine cellar. But the problem was, this wine cellar wasn't good enough or big enough. I never saw it, though I once saw another one which was very small. It was the size of a closet, but I was still impressed. But I did taste some of their wine one time. I can't really tell the difference, though, between a bottle of wine that costs $100, or even $30, and a bottle that costs $500. At that dinner they might have been serving wine that cost even more than that. Not for me, especially, but for some of the other guests. I'm sure that very expensive wines are really wasted on most people, including myself. I was quite young at the time, but even now a very expensive wine would be wasted on me, probably. This couple learned that if they enlarged the wine cellar and improved it in certain other specific ways, their insurance premiums would be lower. They thought this was a good idea, even though it would cost something, initially, to make these improvements. The bulldozer and other machinery and labor that I saw out the window of the place where I was living at the time, which was a house borrowed from a friend who was also a friend of theirs, must have been costing them in the thousands, but I'm sure the money they spent on it was earned back within a few years or even one year by their savings on the premiums. So I can see this was a prudent move on their part. It was a move that anyone could make concerning some other thing, not necessarily a wine cellar. The point is that any improvement that will eventually save money is a good idea. This is long in the past by now. They must have saved quite a lot altogether, over the years, from the changes they made. So many years have gone by, though, that they have probably sold the house by now. Maybe the improved wine cellar raised the price of the house and they earned back even more money. I was not just young but very young when I watched the bulldozer out my window. The noise did not really bother me very much, because there were so many other things bothering me when I tried to work. In fact, I probably welcomed the sight of the bulldozer. I was impressed by their wine, and by the good paintings they also owned. They were nice, friendly people, but I didn't think much of their clothes or furniture. I spent a lot of time looking out the window and thinking about them. I don't know what that was worth. It was probably a waste of my time. Now I'm a lot older. But here I am, still thinking about them. There are a lot of other things that I've forgotten, but I haven't forgotten them or their fire insurance. I must have thought I could learn something from them.

Mother's Reaction to
My Travel Plans

Gainsville! It's too bad your *cousin* is dead!

For Sixty Cents

You are in a Brooklyn coffee shop, you have ordered only one cup of coffee, and the coffee is sixty cents, which seems expensive to you. But it is not so expensive when you consider that for this same sixty cents you are renting the use of one cup and saucer, one metal cream pitcher, one plastic glass, one small table, and two small benches. Then, to consume if you want to, besides the coffee and the cream, you have water with ice cubes and, in their own dispensers, sugar, salt, pepper, napkins, and ketchup. In addition, you can enjoy, for an indefinite length of time, the air conditioning that keeps the room at a perfectly cool temperature, the powerful white electric light that lights every corner of the room so that there are no shadows anywhere, the view of the people passing outside on the sidewalk in the hot sunlight and wind, and the company of the people inside, who are laughing and turning endless variations on one rather cruel joke at the expense of a little balding redheaded woman sitting at the counter and dangling her crossed feet from the stool, who tries to reach out with her short, white arm and slap the face of the man standing nearest to her.

How Shall I Mourn Them?

Shall I keep a tidy house, like L.?

Shall I develop an unsanitary habit, like K.?

Shall I sway from side to side a little as I walk, like C.?

Shall I write letters to the editor, like R.?

Shall I retire to my room often during the day, like R.?

Shall I live alone in a large house, like B.?

Shall I treat my husband coldly, like K.?

Shall I give piano lessons, like M.?

Shall I leave the butter out all day to soften, like C.?

Shall I have problems with typewriter ribbons, like K.?

Shall I have a strong objection to the drinking of juice, like K.?

Shall I hold many grudges, like B.?

Shall I buy large loaves of white bread from the baker, like C.?

Shall I keep tubs of clams in my freezer, like C.?

Shall I make a bad pun at the wrong moment, like R.?

Shall I read detective novels in bed at night, like C.?

Shall I take beautiful care of my own person, like L.?

Shall I smoke and drink heavily, like K.?

Shall I drink heavily and smoke sometimes, like C.?

Shall I welcome people into my house to visit and to stay, like C.?

Shall I be well informed about many things, like K.?

Shall I know the classics, like K.?

Shall I write letters by hand, like B.?

Shall I write "Dearest Both," like C.?

Shall I use many exclamation marks and capitals, like C.?

Shall I include a poem in my letter, like B.?

Shall I often look up words in the dictionary, like R.?

Shall I admire the picture of the beautiful President of Iceland, like R.?

Shall I often look up etymologies, like R.?

Shall I bring a potted tulip to the back door as a gift, like L.?

Shall I give small dinner parties, like M.?

Shall I get a little arthritis in my hands, like C.?

Shall I keep a gray dove and a gray hound, like L.?

Shall I play the radio by my bed all night, like C.?

Shall I leave too much food in the rented house at the end of the summer, like C.?

Shall I often eat a single baked potato for my dinner, like Dr. S.?

Shall I have ice cream once a year, like Dr. S.?

Shall I swim in the bay alone, even in the worst weather, like C.?

Shall I drink vegetable cooking water, like C.?

Shall I label my folders in shaky handwriting, like R.?

Shall I chew my food slowly and thoroughly, like Dr. S.?

Shall I walk by the canal, like B.?

Shall I take my guests along the canal, like B.?

Shall I put daylily buds in the salad for my guests, like B.?

Shall I come out in the morning neatly dressed with my bed made, like R.?

Shall I have my first cup of coffee at eleven o'clock, like R.?

Shall I lay out the forks in a fan, and the napkins in a row, for company, like L.?

Shall I make pancakes in the morning when traveling, like C.?

Shall I carry liquor in the trunk of my car when on holiday, like C.?

Shall I make an oyster stew on New Year's Eve that is full of sand, like C.?

Shall I hand a knife carefully to another person handle first, like R.?

Shall I speak against my husband to the grocer, like C.?

Shall I always read with a pencil in my hand, like R.?

Shall I hug my bereaved children too long and too often, like C.?

Shall I ignore health warnings, like B.?

Shall I give gifts of money freely, like C.?

Shall I give gifts with animal themes, like C.?

Shall I keep a small plastic seal in my refrigerator, like C.?

Shall I have trouble sleeping on my arm, like R.?

Shall I take off my shirt just before I die, like B.?

Shall I wear only black and white, like M.?

A Strange Impulse

I looked down on the street from my window. The sun shone and the shopkeepers had come out to stand in the warmth and watch the people go by. But why were the shopkeepers covering their ears? And why were the people in the street running as if pursued by a terrible specter? Soon everything returned to normal: the incident had been no more than a moment of madness during which the people could not bear the frustration of their lives and had given way to a strange impulse.

How She Could Not Drive

She could not drive if there were too many clouds in the sky. Or rather, if she could drive with many clouds in the sky, she could not have music playing if there were also passengers in the car. If there were two passengers, as well as a small caged animal, and many clouds in the sky, she could listen but not speak. If a wind blew shavings from the small animal's cage over her shoulder and lap as well as the shoulder and lap of the man next to her, she could not speak to anyone or listen, even if there were very few clouds in the sky. If the small boy was quiet, reading his book in the back seat, but the man next to her opened his newspaper so wide that its edge touched the gearshift and the sunlight shone off its white page into her eyes, then she could not speak or listen while trying to enter a large highway full of fast-moving cars, even if there were no clouds in the sky.

Then, if it was night and the boy was not in the car, and the small caged animal was not in the car, and the car was empty of boxes and suitcases where before it had been full, and the man next to her was not reading a newspaper but looking out the window straight ahead, and the sky was dark so that she could see no clouds, she could listen but not talk, and she could have no music playing, if a motel brightly illuminated above her on a dark hill some distance ahead and to the left seemed to be floating across the highway in front as she drove at high speed between dotted lines with headlights coming at her on the left and up behind her in the rearview mirror and taillights ahead in a gentle curve around to the right underneath the massive airship of motel lights floating across the highway from left to right in front of her, or could talk, but only to say one thing, which went unanswered.

Suddenly Afraid

because she couldn't write the name of what she was: a wa wam owm
owamn womn

Getting Better

I slapped him again because when I was carrying him in my arms he tore my glasses off and hurled them at the grate in the hall. But he wouldn't have done it if I hadn't been so angry already. After that I put him to bed.

Downstairs, I sat on the sofa eating and reading a magazine. I fell asleep there for an hour. I woke up with crumbs on my chest. When I went into the bathroom, I could not look at myself in the mirror. I did the dishes and sat down again in the living room. Before I went to bed I told myself things were getting better. It was true: this day had been better than the day before, and the day before had been better than most of last week, though not much better.

Head, Heart

Heart weeps.
Head tries to help heart.
Head tells heart how it is, again:
You will lose the ones you love. They will all go. But even the
earth will go, someday.
Heart feels better, then.
But the words of head do not remain long in the ears of heart.
Heart is so new to this.
I want them back, says heart.
Head is all heart has.
Help, head. Help heart.

The Strangers

My grandmother and I live among strangers. The house does not seem big enough to hold all the people who keep appearing in it at different times. They sit down to dinner as though they had been expected—and indeed there is always a place laid for them—or come into the drawing room out of the cold, rubbing their hands and exclaiming over the weather, settle by the fire and take up a book I had not noticed before, continuing to read from a place they had marked with a worn paper bookmark. As would be quite natural, some of them are bright and agreeable, while others are unpleasant—peevish or sly. I form immediate friendships with some—we understand each other perfectly from the moment we meet—and look forward to seeing them again at breakfast. But when I go down to breakfast they are not there; often I never see them again. All this is very unsettling. My grandmother and I never mention this coming and going of strangers in the house. But I watch her delicate pink face as she enters the dining room leaning on her cane and stops in surprise—she moves so slowly that this is barely perceptible. A young man rises from his place, clutching his napkin at his belt, and goes to help her into her chair. She adjusts to his presence with a nervous smile and a gracious nod, though I know she is as dismayed as I am that he was not here this morning and will not be here tomorrow and yet behaves as though this were all very natural. But often enough, of course, the person at the table is not a polite young man but a thin spinster who eats silently and quickly and leaves before we are done, or an old woman who scowls at the rest of us and spits the skin of her baked apple onto the edge of her plate. There is nothing we can do about this. How can we get rid of people we never invited who leave of their own accord anyway, sooner or later? Though we are of different generations, we were both brought up never to ask questions and only to smile at things we did not understand.

The Busy Road

I am so used to it by now
that when the traffic falls silent,
I think a storm is coming.

Order

All day long the old woman struggles with her house and the objects in it: the doors will not shut; the floorboards separate and the clay squeezes up between them; the plaster walls dampen with rain; bats fly down from the attic and invade her wardrobe; mice make nests in her shoes; her fragile dresses fall into tatters from their own weight on the hanger; she finds dead insects everywhere. In desperation she exhausts herself sweeping, dusting, mending, caulking, gluing, and at night sinks into bed holding her hands over her ears so as not to hear the house continue to subside into ruin around her.

The Fly

At the back of the bus,
inside the bathroom,
this very small illegal passenger,
on its way to Boston.

Traveling with Mother

1.

The bus said "Buffalo" on the front, after all, not "Cleveland." The backpack was from the Sierra Club, not the Audubon Society.

They had said that the bus with "Cleveland" on the front would be the right bus, even though I wasn't going to Cleveland.

2.

The backpack I had brought with me for this was a very sturdy one. It was even stronger than it needed to be.

I practiced many answers to their possible question about what I was carrying in my backpack. I was going to say, "It is sand for potting plants" or "It is for an aromatherapy cushion." I would also have told the truth. But they did not search the luggage this time.

3.

In my rolling suitcase I had the metal container, well wrapped in clothes. That was now her home, or her bed.

I had not wanted to put her in the rolling suitcase. I thought that riding on my back she would at least be near my head.

4.

We waited for the bus. I ate an apple so old it was nearly baked like a pie apple.

I don't know if she, too, heard and was bothered by the recorded announcement. It came over the loudspeaker every few minutes. The bad grammar in the beginning is what would have bothered her: "Due to security reasons . . ."

5.

Leaving the city felt so final that I thought for a moment my money wouldn't be good where we were going.

Before, she could not leave her house. Now she is moving.

6.

It has been so long since she and I traveled together.

There are so many places we could go.

Index Entry

Christian, I'm not a

My Son

This is my husband, and this tall woman with him in the doorway is his new wife. But if he is silly with his new wife, and younger, then I become older, and he is also my son, though he once was older than I, and was my brother, in a smaller family. She, being younger even than he, is now a daughter to me, or a daughter-in-law, though she is taller than I. But if she is smarter than a young woman, and wiser, she is no longer so young, and if wiser than I, she is my older sister, so that he, if still my son, must be her nephew. But if he, very tall though she even taller, has a child who is also my child, am I then not only a mother but also a grandmother and she a great-aunt, if my sister, or an aunt, if my daughter? And has my son then run off with his child's aunt or, worse, his own?

Example of the Continuing Past Tense in a Hotel Room

Your housekeeper *has been* Shelly.

Cape Cod Diary

I listen to the different boats' horns, hoping to learn what kind of boat I'm hearing and what the signal means: is the boat leaving or entering the harbor; is it the ferry, or a whale-watching boat, or a fishing boat? At 5:33 p.m. there is a blast of two deep, resonant notes a major third apart. On another day there is the same blast at 12:54 p.m. On another, at exactly 8:00 a.m.

The boats seem to come and go at all hours, and last night I could still hear their engines sounding well into the early morning. The pier is so far away, though, that the boats are the size of dominoes and their engines can be heard only when the town is quiet.

I am staying by the harbor in a damp little blue-and-white room that smells faintly of gas from the stove. The only people I see are an old couple who live just outside town. Sometimes they have visitors as old as they are, and then they invite me to have dinner or tea with them.

I work in the mornings and early afternoon, then I go out to get my mail. If I shop, I might buy a pencil sharpener, a folder, some paper, and a postcard. Another day, I might buy some fruit, some crackers, and a newspaper.

It is the beginning of August. I am not sure I should stay for the whole month. This may be a good place to work. My neighbors are quiet and I do not even have a telephone. Still, I'm not sure. I am trying to plan out how it would be. I can work most of the day. I can visit the two old people. I can write many letters. I can walk to the library. I can swim. What is missing?

A storm is coming, and the gulls cry over the streets. They have come over the land away from the storm. There is a heavy smell of fish in the air.

A short gust of wind, then calm, then the sea is dark gray and the rain comes down hard, and the wind blows against the awnings. My neighbor in the room above goes to his door, then begins walking around over my head.

To get to the beach from my room I go down the narrow boardwalk between two wooden buildings, mine and the motel next door. The two buildings lean together above me as I pass the windows of the motel apartments, waist high; at certain hours women are working in the kitchens, and there are snatches of conversations in the living rooms. These people seem louder and at the same time more stationary because they are idle and on vacation.

The different groups of people here: the year-round residents, who are sometimes artists and often shop owners; the tourists, who come in couples and families and are generally large, young, healthy, tanned, and polite; of these tourists, most are American, but some are French Canadian, and of these, some do not speak English; Portuguese fishermen, but they are harder to discover; some Portuguese who are not fishermen but whose fathers or grandfathers were fishermen; some fishermen who are not Portuguese.

I looked at whale jawbones in the museum this morning. Then I did some shopping. Whenever I go into the drugstore it seems that many people are buying condoms and motion sickness medicine.

Fog comes in over the next hill, foghorns sound, now and then boats whistle. Waves of mist blow like curtains, or smoke.

The noises here at different times of day: At 5:00 a.m., when sunlight pours into this room, there is relative quiet that continues until after 8:30. Then there is increasing noise from the street: after 10:00 a.m., a gentle Central American music, constant, inoffensive plucking and pinging, as well as the sound of passing cars, voices in conversation, the clatter of silverware from an upstairs terrace restaurant across the street, car engines turning over in the parking lot to one side of my room, people calling out to each other, laughing and talking, and all of this then continues through the day and the evening and past midnight.

I will probably not think about the whale jawbones once I am home again. I have noticed that it is only when I am at the seaside, for one short period of the year, though not every year, that the things of the sea become interesting to me—the shells, the creatures, even the sea-weed; the boats and how they are built and what their functions are; and nautical history, including the history of whaling. Then, when my visit is over, I go away and I don't think about them.

For two days I did not speak to anyone, except to ask for my mail at the post office and say hello to the friendly checkout woman at the small supermarket.

When the storm began today I heard the footsteps of the man who lives above me going across to the door that leads out to his deck, pausing there for a while, and coming away again. The ceiling is low, and the sound of these footsteps is a very loud crunch, so that I feel they are almost on my head. When he comes home, first I hear the clanging of the street gate, then his brisk steps down the concrete walk of the alley, then the hollow wooden clatter as he climbs the stairs inside the building, then the loud crunch over my head. Steps in one direction, steps in another, then steps crisscrossing over my ceiling. Then there is silence—he may be reading or lying down. I know he also paints and sculpts, and when I hear the radio going I think that is what he is doing.

He is a friendly man in late middle age with a loyal group of friends. I discovered this one of the first nights I was here. He had been away in the city for a few days celebrating his aunt's hundredth birthday, as I heard him tell his friends, and was loudly welcomed back by a hoarse-voiced, middle-aged woman trailing a string of other people standing outside our building in the alley. They had come by to see if he was back. I know he is friendly because of a smile and greeting he gave me on his way into the building once, a greeting that lifted my spirits.

Sometimes there are loud thumps from above. At other times he seems to be standing still, and there is something a little mysterious and disturbing in the stillness, since I have trouble imagining what he is doing. Sometimes I hear just a few notes from a saxophone, the same notes repeated the same way a few times or just once before he stops and does not play again, as though something were wrong with the instrument.

There are two buildings on this property, one fronting the street and the other behind it, by the beach, with a small garden in between. My low, ground-floor room does not look out on the beach but on the damp garden. Each house is divided into apartments or rooms, maybe six in all. The landlady sells antique jewelry from a store in the building on the street. Most of the people who live in the buildings have seasonal work here and come to these rooms every summer. They are all quiet and sober, as the landlady made very clear before I moved in. She calls my room an apartment, even though it is just a room, as though there were something vulgar about the word *room*.

I was wrong about my neighbor upstairs. He is not the friendly man who once greeted me. He is barely polite. He has silver hair and a silver goatee and an unpleasant expression around his bulbous nose.

I was also wrong about the saxophone, which is not played by the man upstairs but by my neighbor across the patch of garden, a woman with a dog.

All week long I had heard people saying there would be a storm. I went out onto the beach, into its first fury, to see it hit the water. After I had stood for a while sheltering my face under my hand and watching the buildings on the piers in the distance vanish behind the curtains and sheets of rain, I went down to the water's edge, where the wind was much stronger, to see more closely how the rain hit the water. A man in a yellow slicker was dragging a rowboat up onto the sand. The wind came in so hard that it lifted the rowboat and turned it over. It lifted and flung the sand against my legs, stinging them. I took shelter under the motel deck next door, which is up on stilts off the beach. On the deck over my head, plastic chairs were being slung around and tumbled into corners by the wind.

Now the rain is coming down steadily, and the streets, which were empty at the beginning of the storm, are filling with people again, and there is, again, a heavy fish smell in the air. I have hung my clothes to dry from nails in the beams and posts of my room, so that it is a forest of damp garments swaying in the gusts of wind from the door and the windows.

The essay is taking shape now. As the time passes here, time is passing in the travels of the French historian. I trace and describe his itinerary through this country; he progresses, I progress in the essay, and the days pass. I am coming to feel that he is more my companion, in this room, than the live people in this town. This morning, for instance, because in my imagination I had been traveling with him ever since dawn, I felt I was not here in this seaside town but in a damp river valley some hundreds of miles to the west of here. I was in the previous century. This morning, the historian was watching fireworks from a boat in the middle of a broad river. For him it was evening.

It is not an easy piece of writing. I understand the information in the sources I am using, but I have no general background knowledge to draw on. I am afraid it will be very easy for me to make a mistake.

From within the town I look out at the harbor and across the harbor to the sea beyond. The horizon is very far away. But that view itself, because it hardly changes, becomes a sort of confinement. The streets, too, teeming with people, seem always the same. I feel as though I were knocking up against myself at every turn. I am sometimes almost in a panic. That may be because I am also knocking up against the limits of what I can do with this work.

Yesterday I went a little way out of town, far enough to leave the houses behind. I walked past low hills covered with scrub brush and dead oaks, and dunes covered with dune grass, and then a marsh of bright green reeds cut through with channels of clear water.

But I can see that this, though it was so fresh to me today, and such a relief, would become dull, too, if I watched it from my window every day from a house outside town, and then I would need a glimpse of what I can see here: the stone breakwater, the two piers stretching out into the water, the small boats all pointing the same way, the one big, old hulk beached at low tide and leaning to one side; and in the streets the thick crowds constantly stopping at shop windows; the carriages and horses with women drivers wearing men's formal black suits, their blond hair in topknots; the motley people in a row on the bench before the town hall watching the others walk and drive by; the tall black transvestite who strides up the street in a sequin-covered red dress away from the Crown and Anchor Hotel; the tall white transvestite who stands next to the hotel with his dress open over one lean leg all the way up to his hip, a creased angry look about his long nose under his wig and above his red lips. They are advertising a show at the hotel.

The hotel is a large establishment almost directly across from the plain and tranquil old Unitarian Universalist Meeting House, which is set back from the busy street over an unadorned rectangle of lawn. The church was built in 1874 and is now being restored with the help of a fund raised by a group of painters here. The painters are the most famous inhabitants of this place, along with the writers. Earlier inhabitants were: the Portuguese fishermen and occasional Breton and English fishermen; the whalers; the Pilgrims who first landed here in 1620 and did not stay for three reasons, only two of which I can remember—the harbor was not deep enough and the Indians were not friendly; before them the Nauset and Pamet Indians themselves.

Today in the late afternoon I went to have a beer in the outdoor café next to the small public library, which is an old house shaded by an old oak with a circular wooden bench around its thick trunk. The waiter asked me, "Is there one in your party?" Edith Piaf was singing in the background. I said "Yes" and he brought my beer.

I am thinking about a recent mystery: On the day of the storm something washed ashore that was smooth, rubbery, and the size and shape of a dolphin's nose, though not the right color. It might have been the back of an upholstered plastic seat from a boat. For a day or two it remained there, moving as the water moved it, sometimes in the water and sometimes on the sand, always in about the same place. Then I didn't see it for a few days. Today as I was lying on the beach, a man in a ranger's uniform went under the deck of the motel, dragged the thing out, and methodically tore it to pieces, separating it into different layers. Some layers he left lying on the sand, the rest of it he folded and carried away with him.

The faces of the tourists here reflect what they see all day long, the harbor, the old buildings, the other people in the streets, with openness, even wonder. Only when they look in the shop windows, and seem to consider buying something, do they lose some of their ease and joy. Their faces close into expressions of intentness, care, even exhaustion.

I have been with the old people again. It is restful to me after I have been working, though if the work has not gone well I will not see them at all, preferring to sit with the difficulty than to leave it behind.

When I have made a little progress I am glad to leave it and have their company. In contrast to the work, to the denseness of all the information I am trying to put in some order, their conversation is undemanding. The old woman will talk endlessly if I ask her a question or two; the old man listens to her and sometimes adds a brief comment of his own. They do not seem to notice if I do not talk. Nothing at all is required of me when one says to the other, "Did you take your pills?"

The old man often sits in the passenger seat of the car waiting for his wife to return from doing an errand. He tells me he likes to watch the people going past. He will wait almost any length of time if he can watch the people and think his thoughts, which he finds interesting. Today he saw three women approach together, one of them feeble-minded, as he called her, her head bobbing constantly. The leader of the group stopped by the hood of his car, set a pile of papers down on it, and began searching her purse for something. She took a long time searching and the old man sat there watching her directly in front of him and also watching the feeble-minded woman, who stood at the edge of the sidewalk all that time, her head bobbing.

At the end of one pier tonight, two men were casting far out for blue-fish. One remarked to the other that the slapping of the lure on the water over and over might be frightening the fish. At the other pier, fishing boats were lined up side by side, thick clumps of nets hanging from the masts, dinghies tied down onto the tops of cabins, stacks of new wooden crates on the decks, along with piles of baskets—only what was needed for the work.

From the beach, at dusk, I look back at the land and I see steeples against the sky, and, on a roof, what look like four white statues of women in robes against the sky, as in a cemetery, but then look more carefully and see that they are four white folded beach umbrellas with large knobs on top. In the water, small boats all point the same way on their moorings, only one suddenly will move independently, wandering a little and turning.

At night the Unitarian Universalist church burns a light in its steeple in remembrance of those lost at sea.

At the entrance of the alley, my alley, where it opens into the street, as at the mouth of a stream, there is the life of the street, turbulent, eddying, restlessly moving into the early hours of the morning.

At dawn I was woken by a thrashing in the patch of garden outside my door. It was a skunk caught in some brambles.

The travels of my French historian have taken him away from the damp river valley and out to the Midwest now. He is studying the structures of municipal governments in newly incorporated towns. This interests me only a little, but the historian himself is good company, and so his intelligence illuminates these subjects and they become tolerable.

Yesterday I took a walk in the rain and saw: tough-stemmed old stalks of Queen Anne's lace with their several heads waving in the wind and banging against a gravestone; the cemetery that has been allowed to go wild and is posted with signs prohibiting overnight camping; a woman awkwardly turning her car in a dead-end lane and crushing some tall stands of purple loosestrife outside a fenced garden; the man in the garden on his knees weeding a flower bed; a uniformed nurse in a small paddock talking over the fence about her horse to a neighbor in the road; the oldest house in town, built of wood from wrecked ships, with a plaque in front of it describing its circular brick cellar, whose technical name was included, though I now forget what it was; a street called Mechanic Street.

Last Sunday I decided to go to church. It didn't matter to me which one I went to. I was on my way to the Catholic church, St. Peter's, with its onion-shaped steeple of dark painted wood, when the bell began to toll in the belfry of the Unitarian Universalist church; I was walking slightly uphill in a narrow lane where I could see the belfry close at hand; I changed my mind and went back down the lane, into the yard past the flea market on the front lawn, into the church building, and upstairs to the chapel itself with its trompe l'oeil interior. Even the columns that looked so real were not real columns; the sparse congregation and the minister might have been trompe l'oeil, too.

But the minister was a young woman from the Harvard Divinity School, full of information, with an emphatic and direct manner; the music played on the organ was well chosen and performed; the soloist sang well from the organ loft; and the hymns were familiar old ones. Downstairs, after the service, sweet lemonade was served, with rounds of toast covered with sliced egg and olives laid out on a table that stood between the door to the musty basement thrift shop and the outer doorway with its rectangle of bright sunlight.

Later, on the street, I was thinking about a funny story the minister had told. A bronzed man on a motorcycle with impenetrable dark glasses and a bandanna around his forehead passed me and gave me a long dark look. I had been smiling, inadvertently, at him.

Recent dreams about animals: I was about to take an exam given by Z. when a small animal, a shrew or a mouse, escaped and I went off to help catch it. At that point I discovered other loose animals, larger ones. I alerted people and tried to get the animals back into their cages. This was taking place in a school, and the animals were probably connected with the exam.

On another night I was the one who let four animals loose in a field—a brown-and-white goat, a palomino horse, and two other large animals whose descriptions I was going to advertise so that they could be recovered. I stood watching the horse gallop into the field among other horses.

Yesterday I was sitting in the back seat of the old people's car. We were driving out to the ocean beach. The old man made a statement that shocked me, though neither he nor the old woman noticed it. I sat there shocked behind the old woman, who had great trouble driving straight into the setting sun.

I go for a long walk on a railroad track near the old people's house. The rails have been taken up, and the bed is straight and narrow and visible ahead of me for a great distance. A thin, bearded man dressed in layers of ragged clothing comes ambling along toward me with his black dog, which ranges around him nosing in the underbrush. The old people's cat, which has been walking with me, turns broadside to the dog and arches its back.

Last night, after midnight, walking barefoot near the kitchen sink, I stepped on something slippery and hard. On the mat lay what looked like some animal part, a glistening innard of uniform color and texture. I bent down to examine it: it was a slug. I was afraid I had killed it. I picked it up: it was cool and moist. As I held it in my palm, this dollop of glistening muscle, two bumps appeared at one end of it and then grew steadily into two long horns, as below them symmetrically two more bumps grew into slighter protrusions which I guessed were eyes, and at the same time the body thinned out and tensed, and then the slug set off and glided around my wrist and up my arm.

Tonight I heard the footsteps of a neighbor returning down the concrete path, then more footsteps, then many more all at once, and they continued so long and so steadily that I realized they were not footsteps: it was the rain. Heavy drops splashed on the leaves in the garden and on the planks of the wooden decks. Then, among the splashes of rain, I did hear the footsteps of a neighbor coming home, and it was the man above me, now walking over my ceiling.

Yesterday I rode a bicycle along a winding macadam trail past lily-choked ponds and through a thin forest of young beeches. On my way back, I stopped on the pier to watch fishermen mending their nets before they set out to sea. They pull large comblike implements through the squares of the net and tie knots in it. One man holds the net while the other does the mending with quick, economical motions. Small clusters of tourists stand on the pier above looking down at them respectfully where they work in the boats.

Not far away, three men fished off the pier for mackerel, casting again and again, pulling up silver fish that fought hard, all muscle, then unhooking them and slipping them carefully into a Styrofoam cooler where they flopped so violently that the cooler shook and thudded for a while after it was closed.

At the same time, a bright red oil truck was fueling the boats. It would stop next to them on the pier where they were tied two or three deep alongside and send the long hose down into one, over one into the next, and then into the third. At the same time, a steel cable that extended the length of the pier into what seemed to be a fish-packing shed was being wound mechanically onto a drum in one of the fishing boats. The winding went on and on. A group of tourists watched this carefully, too.

The tourists took pictures of the fishermen mending their nets. If a tourist asked a fisherman to smile, the fisherman would glance up soberly, with a neutral expression on his face, and keep still for the picture, but he would not smile.

I went out to eat recently with the two old people and two old friends of theirs. We sat in a room surrounded by water and they all ordered lobster. The plates came, and the red lobsters looked pretty lying on their lettuce leaves next to their little white cups of melted butter. Now the conversation died and the table was silent except for the furious cracking, pulling, and prying of those old people, who suddenly showed such competent physical strength, intent on destroying their lobsters.

People I see here: the clerk at the post office; the friendly checkout woman at the supermarket; my neighbors; my landlady; the woman across the garden, who once asked me in a neutral, curious tone what I was doing here; last night, a plump, gregarious off-duty bartender attending the free movie at the public library, though I did not speak to him. He wore a bandanna tied around his forehead and cowboy boots. He was there to see the 1954 movie, whose title I forget. Most of the small audience were old people calling back and forth to each other.

"Everybody's here!" someone cried.

I felt I was included in "everybody," though I was sitting by myself waiting for the movie to begin. I listened to the bartender talk to the other people. Then we all watched the movie.

A plumber came to my room yesterday to fix the shower. He told me his family had lived here for generations. He said that these days there isn't much cod or haddock and the fishermen are taking shellfish off the Great Bank about six miles west of the tip of the land; the beds there seem to be inexhaustible.

I have seen great crates of these shellfish, which I thought were quahogs, coming up onto the pier, hoisted by a small crane on a boat. The crates were stacked on the wharf while tractor trailers from Maryland with their engines running prepared to load them. Seagulls ran around on the asphalt with their wings raised threatening one another over the scraps. Only one gull sat on a crate at the top of a stack and pulled the slimy, elastic flesh of a quahog up through the slats, leaning back as he pulled, bending forward to get another grip, and leaning back again in the midst of a great noise from the boat's engines.

This was at twilight, and as the sky darkened, the lights on the boats grew brighter, and a handful of tourists watched, standing gingerly at the edge of the pier. The young fishermen, barechested, wearing shorts and high rubber boots, went about their work steadily, maneuvering hooks, hoisting a dredger, then a large piece of grating. The boat's engine throbbed, sometimes thundered.

On another night it was later. I was the only one watching. Sparks flew up into the darkness from a boat where something was being welded or soldered. Another boat set out to sea after blowing its whistle. A black fisherman ran to the stern of the boat as it pulled away. He looked up, smiled, and waved.

I have just come back from looking at the motorcycles on the pier. They are parked side by side in great numbers near the snack bars that sell such surprisingly good Portuguese fish soup. They are of all kinds, plain and fancy. The fancy ones are decorated with antlers, and with leopard skins.

More crickets are singing now as the air grows colder and colder. It is the last day of August and the season is changing suddenly. Just as it is time for me to leave, the historian, too, has finished his tour and will be returning to Europe.

Almost Over:
What's the Word?

He says,
"When I first met you
I didn't think you would turn out to be so
. . . strange."

A Different Man

At night he was a different man. If she knew him as he was in the morning, at night she hardly recognized him: a pale man, a gray man, a man in a brown sweater, a man with dark eyes who kept his distance from her, who took offense, who was not reasonable. In the morning, he was a rosy king, gleaming, smooth-cheeked and smooth-chinned, fragrant with perfumed talc, coming out into the sunlight with a wide embrace in his royal red plaid robe . . .

DAVID IGNASZEWSKI

LYDIA DAVIS

VARIETIES OF DISTURBANCE

Lydia Davis's story collections include *Samuel Johnson Is Indignant*, a *Village Voice* favorite, and *Almost No Memory*, a *Los Angeles Times* Best Book of the Year. The acclaimed translator of the new *Swann's Way*, by Marcel Proust, and recipient of a 2003 MacArthur Fellowship, she teaches at SUNY Albany, where she is also a Fellow of the New York State Writers Institute.

"ALL WHO KNOW [DAVIS'S] WORK PROBABLY REMEMBER THEIR FIRST TIME READING IT. IT KIND OF BLOWS THE ROOF OFF OF SO MANY OF OUR ASSUMPTIONS ABOUT WHAT CONSTITUTES SHORT FICTION. I READ IT ON THE F TRAIN FROM 6TH AVENUE TO PARK SLOPE—IT'S A LONG RIDE AND THAT BOOK ISN'T ALL THAT LONG—AND BY THE END I FELT LIBERATED. SHE'D BROKEN ALL OF THE MOST CONSTRAINING RULES. SOME OF HER STORIES HAVE PLOTS BUT MOST DON'T. SOME ARE IN THE RANGE OF ACCEPTABLE SHORT STORY LENGTH, MOST AREN'T. MANY STRADDLE A LINE BETWEEN PHILOSOPHY, POETRY AND FICTION, CATEGORIES THAT SEEM MEANINGLESS BECAUSE HER STORIES JUST WORK. THERE IS RARELY A PLOT AS WE EXPECT FROM PLOT. THE CHARACTERS IN THE COURSE OF THE STORY DON'T UNDERGO A FUNDAMENTAL CHANGE. THE PLOT, RATHER, STEMS FROM THE NARRATOR'S TRYING TO GET AT SOME TRUTH. [DAVIS'S] STORIES ARE AS OFTEN AS NOT MENTAL EXERCISES, A BRAIN TRYING TO CONCLUDE. BECAUSE TRUTH IS WHAT SHE'S AFTER. THERE IS AN UNRELENTING AND MERCILESS TRUTH PRESENTED, OR AT LEAST FUMBLED FOR, IN EVERYTHING [SHE] WRITES . . . DAVIS IS ONE OF THE MOST PRECISE AND ECONOMICAL WRITERS WE HAVE."—DAVE EGGERS, McSWEENEY'S